FALLOUT

Craig Lefebvre

ISBN: 9781734905885
Copyright © 2022
Published by: Dimensional Healings

Editors:
Risa Rodgers
Jillian H. Smith
Jill Behme Conaway
Kathleen Schurman
Michelle Behme

Creative director: John Chadziewicz
Concept and design: Craig Lefebvre
Book cover & layout: Word-2-Kindle.com

In memory of Diane

FALLOUT was inspired by true events...

The truth is stranger than strange itself.

Contents

PART I

Haunted by the past.

The old man stood before the bathroom mirror, slowly he wiped away the blood that was running from his nose, while looking into his own two pail blue eyes. Memories, like a dream, came flooding back. There were flashes of light, black almond-shaped eyes, and cold steel surgical tools sitting out in plain sight before him. He thought to himself that it was like having a dream within a dream when this happened. The only comfort he found in this was that it was at least familiar to him, though he could never get used to it. There was anxiety too, even if he was always returned unharmed. Sometimes he wasn't even aware that he had been taken, until he examined his body after taking a shower in the morning; it was common to have bruises on his wrists and hands and impressions left behind on the skin of his pail white ankles. As he took his shirt off, he noticed an obvious strap mark that was left behind. In most cases, he would simply black out as soon as he saw "THEM," and why they couldn't simply come during the light of day, was a mystery to him? The dark of night made this exchange a hundred times worse. It wasn't fear of the unknown any more, but rather a fear of knowing.

Sometimes when he watched science programs on TV in the evening, he would have flashbacks, and have to shut the program off. These type of memories are like dead bodies being dumped into a river called life. Somewhere or somehow, they always float to the surface as memories. A man cannot run away from himself, no matter how hard he tries. Everyday you get up and do it all over again. What choice do we have? He even thought about eating a bullet once or twice, but then conceded that it was a coward's move. Even the ritual of making his own bed stirred his anxiety. He would remember being a small boy, so very clear in his mind, seeing "THEM" at the foot of his bed. Then it all went black. In the morning he would wake up with crusted blood on both his pillow and his face.

A soft humming noise swept over his body causing a quick full-body paralysis. The mind was awake, as the body lay immobilized. The humming reminded him of his time in the Navy, where he served as a plumber, working in the bowels of the vessel. Some nights as the boat ran its radar tests, a low hum could be heard as the lights dimmed off and on again. He could hear this same noise at night before they came. It almost sounded like a car idling out on the street. Breaking out in a cold sweat, he would often get up and look out the window at night. As hard as he tried, the memory of "THEM" never went away.

Moments earlier, he had awoken to the phone ringing. In a daze, he had reached for it and recognized his own hand by the large scar on the backside; a factory accident that had left him painfully arthritic. Now in his old age, he liked to think of it as the "hands of time."

He answered in a gruff smokers voice, "Hello." The voice on the other end replied, "It's Irv, you been sleeping? A deep exhale came across the phone's speaker. "Guess I was." -Today, Irv was in one of his moods. His demeanor was anxious and showed no patience for Smitty.

"What the fuck you doing sleeping this late in the morning old man?"

"I don't know, feels like I was up all night or something."

"Or something?"

"Yes, or something." And then he noticed blood dripping onto his white cotton t-shirt. Smitty quickly reached for his pocket handkerchief. It was the same style he wore in the paper mill on hot summer days to keep the sweat from his eyes. Some days he even kept a bucket of ice water ready and dipped it in periodically wiping down the nape of his neck. The factory work was brutal but the physicality of the work felt good to him.

The two old men abruptly ended their phone call after making plans to get together and watch the baseball game that afternoon. Irv liked the Red Sox, and Smitty always rooted for the Yankees. These two friends, the Irishman and the Englishman, had met in the service and stayed close friends ever since. They even lived a block away from one another. Like so many servicemen, these two men stood like brothers; they had each other's backs. An unbreakable bond. Even after a night of getting drunk and punching each other stupid, they still remained friends.

As if on cue, Irv walked in the door about twenty minutes before the game started. After their last conversation, there was an unspoken tension in the room. Irv walked past Smitty, not saying a word and put his six pack in the garage refrigerator. It was an old rusted General Electric model, a fifties relic. Smitty stubbornly fixed it whenever it broke down, refusing to let it go. Always the cheap depression era kinda guy. The handle still had some spots of chrome left on it. There was a huge Ford Motor Company sticker on the door. Every time Irv looked at the sticker, he would say to himself, "Fucked-over rebuild Dodge." He was a Chevy man through and through.

Unexpectedly, a voice came from the garage. "What's with all the construction shit on the work table?" There, laid out on a long folding table, was white paste, wallpaper, a metal trowel and a gallon of paint. "I thought you were done with all your remodeling?" After rolling his eyes, Smitty finally replied.

"I wouldn't have invited you over if you were going to be so fucking nosey." A minute passed and Irv was now standing at the room's threshold.

"Oh I see, you're Mr. God Damn Secrets again -right, right, right." With a half smile, Smitty looked at Irv and said, "I've got a secret for yah!" And with that, he grimaced and ripped a loud fart. The two men sat in silence for the next hour, until the phone rang. It rang three or four times until Irv got annoyed enough to ask, "Yah gonna answer it?"

"No, let the machine get it. It's probably a telemarketer anyways." The machine came on after the fifth ring, "Hi, this is Smitty, if you're important, leave a message. If not, go away." There was a long beep before a woman's nervous voice came on the speaker.

"Um, hi Dad it's me, um, please call me back. I um, need a favor. Bye." The voice sounded very desperate and sad like someone who was trapped. Irv looked over at Smitty, and then quickly looked back.

"Not a fucking word" Smitty said. His friend snapped back at him.

"Fine, okay got it, not a word," as he held up his two hands as if to say, "I yield." And so they just sat there in an awkward silence for the rest of the game; both of them inwardly thinking about the voice on the other end of the line, and what she may have needed from her father. There were some painful emotions that hadn't been let out yet. Fences needed to be mended here. Smitty lit a smoke and quietly contemplated to himself. Irv was watching him out of the corner of his eye, still not saying a word. He knew his friend was in for it. Not thinking twice about it, he looked back at Smitty once more and raised his drink.

"Here's to you Mr. Smith"

"And here's to you Mr. White." And Irv just got up and left without another word being spoken. He left his friend to his private emotions. It was more than obvious that he should be left alone.

* *

It was to be the last week of August, with no signs of autumn in the humid morning air. The leaves hadn't quite started to change colors yet. Instead, they were beginning to turn brown and curl upwards at the end of a very long and hot summer drought. A change of season was just beyond the horizon for the small industrial New England State of Connecticut.

On a small outcropping, hidden by the white birches overlooking the Connecticut River, sat an old man who was a veteran and a retired mill worker, and a boy who was thought to be his protege. They remained there for a spell in a familiar silence, watching all the different types of people going by on their boats. All going by, just like the long summer had, like a heavy daydream. Those people on boats, looking so small, all seemed to be worlds apart from them as they went about their daily lives down on the river. The boy's mind drifted to an other-worldly place, as he wondered if any of them had possibly seen the strange things that he had. And did they know about "THEM?", he thought to himself.

He imagined each one of those people having a story to tell but maybe not as exciting as his. Just then pictures of large black eyes swirled in his mind. For a moment, he was right back there in the ship. His heart rate began to accelerate. He remembered only bits and pieces of the few times that they had taken him. And he was totally unsure what to do with these memories now.

Every once in a while the old man looked down at the boy, studying his position in silent observation, while smoke whirled from his full-bent pipe. He was always contemplating the boy's presence in the world, imagining the story that he would share with him one day, the story of "THEM."

After a good amount of time had passed, the old man finally spoke to the boy. "Carl," he said, "I'm going to miss you when you move back to the city with your mom next week." The boy looked up at him with his big, doughy, brown eyes. "Smitty, for real, you're my best friend! Why can't I stay with you? Please!" The old man looked away from the boy, so as not to appear too overly emotional. A tear caught the corner of his eye. In an overtly manly fashion, he pulled out his handkerchief, blew his nose twice, then quickly complained about his damn allergies. "I think it's those cottonwood trees over there." He then grumbled, "The leaf mold is coming, I can smell it in the air."

Some more time passed as the two companions watched the boats going by, some moving fast, some slowly, and a few moving only by sail. Smitty pointed to the off-white sailboat, the one to his far left.

"Ya' see that one over there? My friend, Tom, taught me how to sail one of those when I was in the Navy. I was maybe twenty years old back then, full of myself to boot. And this one time I was busy watching him run the rope, when I was caught off guard by the boom. It hit me hard, and I was laid out flat on the deck. I was knocked out cold. Tom came over to me as I was coming to, and he pointed at me with a giant grin on his face. "You can't fix stupid." You see, Carl, there is a lot of stupid going on in the world right now. People are killing, people are starving and people are pushing each other out of the way to grab more of whatever they think they want. People think the world owes them. And for what?"

The boy chirped back, "What do you mean by that?"

Carl was only eleven years old, and much of their conversations went right over his head. The old man grinned at the boy, and then for the next half hour tried to explain his version of politics. He went on and on about personal rights, freedom of speech, the Constitution, liberty, the American flag and what it all stands for. Before he wrapped up his rant, he stated proudly that he "had served his country, and I don't owe nobody nothin'!"

The boy had lost track of the conversation after about five minutes, but quickly inquired after a long pause: "Where are we having lunch this time, Smitty?"

It was their habit, all summer long, to find a new place for lunch after they completed one of their little adventures. These outings had come to be what Smitty referred to as their "walkabouts." Before each adventure, he liked to say that man needed to go out and observe the natural world to remember why he was in it.

"People forget what their lives are even about. They get up and go to work each and every day and just spin their wheels with no intended purpose." He released a big circle of smoke from his pipe, hoping to accentuate his point. The soft sweet smell of cherry tobacco filled the air. This smell would become one of Carl's favorite memories about the old man.

After another long pause he said, "Carl, we're going to head over to the Blue Oar in Haddam so we can sit on the rocks, eat some clam strips, and watch the world go by some more." The boy briefly hesitated and then agreed to his idea. Secretly, he had wanted hot dogs again, with ketchup and some relish. He remembered making the long trip to another place called Blackies the previous weekend for lunch, where he discovered sweet pepper relish for the first time. Smitty, with his mouth full of food, told the story about how the Blackies building used to belong to the Wolcott Fire Department.

In good faith, Carl trusted Smitty's lunch choices, just going along with whatever it was that the old man said, at least for the most part. On occasion, the boy pushed for pancakes, as they were his favorite food. Here in Connecticut, he also discovered what real maple syrup tasted like. They had once taken a trip over to the small town of Woodbury, so Smitty could sell some of his old antique tools, and they stopped at a local sugar house afterwards for a tour.

At the sugar house, Carl learned how much maple water it took to make the syrup and how the wood fire had to burn for almost two whole days to make the syrup. He preferred the darker grade B syrup to grade A, for its richer taste. The best part for Carl was the free samples after they had listened to the man talk about his "hobby job" for over twenty minutes.

Carl rarely listened to much of what people were saying to him. Mostly, he liked to daydream when the adults were talking. He studied the lines on their faces, thinking about how he too would be that old one day. His mind wandered to his father, as it often did. On what was the worst day of his short life, Carl woke one morning last winter to a note on the kitchen table that just said, "I quit." His parents had a huge argument the night before about money. Even the pillow over his head couldn't muffle the sound of the yelling.

After that, he was a loner child walking in the shadow of only his mother, a single parent, with no guiding light as a male role model. Things changed for the better when he met his newly-discovered grandfather, Smitty. It was for the first time just this past June, the summer of 1984.

Things seemed to move very quickly leading up to his move to Connecticut. Emotionally, he still felt like he was stuck in limbo, isolated in his own thoughts. He didn't know much about trust or love anymore after his dad left. It was Carl's mom, Ms. Susan Smith, an inner-city school teacher, who had to drop him off at Smitty's. It was to be only for the summer, with barely a word of warning from her. Smitty, the old sailor, was Susan's estranged father. She called him at the end of Carl's school year, seemingly out of the blue, after not speaking with him for many, many years. She was pleading for, not just requesting, his help. Smitty could hear her desperation on the phone, and his heart caved in with grief. He couldn't refuse.

It was after Susan's mom had died that she and Smitty had lost touch. After the funeral, words were said, feelings were hurt and they drifted apart in a deserted silence. The tide had left the shore so to speak. After that, she had relocated to New York City for a higher paying job as a math teacher, just outside of Brooklyn. That is where she met Carl's dad, fell in love, but never married him. He could never commit to her for fear of being tied down. It's easy for a man to just walk away when there are no roots or foundation in his life.

2

The month of June was when Susan showed up, exactly when she said she would, at Smitty's door. It was late in the afternoon. She stood there with her boy just waiting; no one answered the doorbell. Totally annoyed, she opened the door to the breezeway only to discover Smitty fast asleep with a beer in one hand and a half-burnt cigarette in the other. This is all while the Yankees vs. Tigers game blared on his old radio that sat on top of his ancient black and white TV set.

Susan then called out to him, "Hey, Dad! Dad... Dad!" Suddenly waking up, he said, "Huh, What, what... what? Oh, you're here."

Then, he seemed to come to life all at once. The beer didn't spill, and the cigarette never left his hand, almost like it was a rehearsed act, or maybe he was just faking his deep slumber to avoid the moment. The truth was that it could have just been from many years of practice. Before he even said a proper hello to them, he asked, "Who won the game?", like nothing else in the world was more important than that. The moment was stolen by his absence of being. Susan, hiding her anger, was secretly grinding her teeth behind closed lips.

The greeting from Susan was rather trite, as Susan appeared to be very short on patience with her dad after his not answering the door. Seeing him like this set off all her old memories, the ones buried deep in her subconscious.

She thought she had grown out of them somehow, but no. The wounds were still fresh in her mind. These memories all held what she didn't like about the old man, all of his bad habits. Given the obvious opportunity, she somehow failed in that moment to forgive him. She also failed in that moment to remember all the good things that he had done for her throughout her life. When she was growing up, the guy never missed a dance recital or any of her sporting events. But, in the history of her wounded pride, none of it seemed to matter anyway. He could have dropped to his knees begging for her forgiveness and she would have just as much shown her indifference to him. It was a measured spite. Old wounds, it seemed, ran deep in this family. Hurt feelings were like scorched earth, and only time would tell if new foundations were to be laid upon that.

Swallowing a mouth full of pride in that moment, she had to "eat crow" as they say, for the sake of her child. We all do on occasion, and that's just part of life and being human after all. Stepping forward into the living room she pushed Carl ahead of her.

"Hi… um hello, father." She was looking down, shuffling her feet.

"Is this the young man you had called me about?"

"Yes," she said. "This is my son, Carl."

Carl, the nervous eleven-year old boy, cautiously approached and said "hi" to the old man. Smitty held out his hand to shake the boy's, only Carl didn't know what to do in the moment. Susan encouraged him.

"Go ahead, Carl, shake your grandfather's hand. He won't bite."

The old man replied, "You can just call me Smitty, that's what everyone else calls me around here."

Reluctantly, the boy approached his grandfather and put his small hand in Smitty's, which was like an old, wrinkled catcher's mitt. This was the hand of a working-class hero, one who had toiled and earned every penny that had ever crossed it. A hand like this was not like that of any lawyer, businessman, preacher, or even the milkman. Smitty had the hand strength of ten men combined after all of his years of being a plumber at the local paper mill.

"This is how real men shake hands, Carl. We'll work on that again tomorrow when we go out for a walk in the afternoon, and I'll show you the neighborhood."

Carl remained silent, not sure what to think of the stranger.

"Everyday you and I will try and have a little adventure together. It will be fun, you'll see. So what is your favorite food, Carl?"

"Pancakes!" the boy finally spoke.

"Okay, we'll go to Cody's, down in New Haven for some pancakes in the morning, but you'll have to get up a little early. And do you like music? Because they have these little jukeboxes at each table that are coin operated." An hour later, the family reunion was broken up by Susan's abrupt departure. In that moment, Carl could have easily protested but instead yielded to the situation at hand. He wanted something better than watching the unspoken pain on his mother's face and the overcrowded boroughs of New York City.

After Susan said her farewells to the boy, she smiled and waved to Smitty; it was an impartial goodbye. There were a few moments of awkward silence between the old man and the boy. Carl just stood there holding his bag of stuff, staring off into nowhere. He was taking in all of his new surroundings. There was a green pleather couch, a single tweed brown armchair, some family photos of people he didn't recognize and a few empty cans of Schlitz on a metal tray table. A vertical wooden tennis racquet had been converted into an ashtray holder next to the chair. The place looked like it had forgotten a woman's touch decades ago. It was obvious that the old man lived alone and was perfectly happy with the "basic" creature comforts. It wasn't dirty, it wasn't clean either, but it did look well lived in.

Smitty observed the boy looking about the room taking study of his old house.

"Do you want me to show you some old photos of the family?" Smitty asked breaking the silence.

"Yes sir, I guess so."

The old man grabbed the boy's bag and tossed it onto the couch.

"We can sort that business out later."

He then started taking down the photos from the wall. The first one was of him back in his Navy days, dressed in his uniform whites, obviously the most proud moment in his life. When he spoke about those past days, he puffed out his chest a little; in his mind he was twenty again. The next was of him and his late wife, Tabitha. "See how much she looks like your mom?" But the old man immediately felt uncomfortable as he noticed the boy's light brown skin. Smitty, feeling awkward, pushed it to the back of his mind and kept on talking.

He then explained to Carl how they had met while he was in the service. "She wasn't like any of the other gals you see. A real looker... she was." It was while he was on shore leave for some R&R when he was stationed down in Virginia that they met. A few years after that he was transferred to Groton, Connecticut. He and Tabitha had kept in touch until he had finished his time in the service. A year later, they married. There was no questioning their love for each other.

Smitty had grown up in Connecticut, so he pushed his new love interest to follow after him and move to the small industrial New England state. He had promised her that he had a steady paycheck every week from the mill and could keep a roof over their heads no matter what. Smitty then looked down at Carl and said, "Women, most of the time, just want to feel safe and taken care of. After that, it's all good." Sitting back in his easy chair, he showed Carl some other pictures of his mother as a child with pigtails. The boy noticed how happy she had looked back then. It was very much unlike the woman she was now.

That night, Smitty made them steak and eggs for dinner. Carl ate up everything in sight, as he had never been offered anything for lunch that afternoon. Later Smitty helped him unpack his very small travel bag. There were only a few items of clothing, comic books, and some toy GI Joe action figures. Smitty got so excited by the sight of the glorious little army men strewn about the bed of his guest room, so much so, that he lost track of time. In that moment, he was caught up in the feelings of remembrance of wanting a son of his own. He didn't know it yet, but this was to be his chance. It was Carl in this room that used to be his daughter's, his new grandson filling this forgotten void. In this room, where he had once wiped away the memory of his daughter after their many years of estrangement, the hands of time were to be reset for a new beginning. Surely a blatant irony for the salty old man and an unforeseen chance from the universe to have purpose in his life once again.

The next morning, Carl woke up at the crack of dawn as he was still on his school schedule. He wandered out into the living room to find the old man asleep in his armchair. The TV was on from the night before. Carl could see that his socks and shoes were still on his feet, like someone had temporarily hit the pause button from where he had left off just the day before.

Carl slowly approached and whispered, "Smitty... heh... Smitty?" The old man slowly opened his eyes and eventually came to. Carl reminded him they were supposed to go out for pancakes. "Yes, I know," replied Smitty. Slowly moving, he shuffled off into the bathroom taking care of the three S's: a shit, a shower and a shave. He donned his usual outfit, which was a pair of brown leather boots, pressed tan khakis and a plaid collared button-down shirt. After Smitty got dressed, he went over to his nightstand, grabbed his wallet, some loose change and a chrome Zippo lighter which was engraved with his old Navy unit logo. The one thing he never had to look for, however, was his thin gold wedding ring. It was impossible to take it off over his old and swollen knuckles.

Thirty minutes later they were in Smitty's old Ford F-150 pickup headed out for some breakfast. Smitty drove like the old man that he was. The silence between them was most awkward as neither one knew what to say to the other. They stopped at the Exxon gas station on the way there, so that the old man could buy a newspaper and a pack of Lucky's. While there, he picked up a New Haven Advocate, the free weekly paper, to see if it had stuff for him to do with the kid during the next week or so.

At the diner, the two cohorts ordered as soon as the young blond waitress arrived at their table. Smitty ordered first with oatmeal, black coffee and bacon. Carl ordered pancakes with chocolate chips and an orange juice. Before they got their food, Carl broke the silence and asked, "How come you tossed a quarter into my room last night Smitty?"

"What quarter?"

"This one, look see…"

Carl held out his hand for Smitty to see, and there he held a well-tarnished centennial quarter. It was marked "D" 1976. The old man smiled at the boy with a foolish grin like he was the only one in on the joke.

"That wasn't me, Carl." Carl was now even more curious.

"What do you mean it wasn't you? It's only the two of us in your house, right?" Smitty held his hand up to his mouth covering a cough that was going to turn into a laugh. Then he said, "Well… not exactly. There is the ghost of my late wife, your deceased grandmother, Tabitha. She comes around every so often and leaves a quarter on my pillow. It's her way of saying "hi" and letting me know that things are okay on the other side. You see we made a deal that if one of us died before the other, we would come back and leave a sign for the other. Carl, just because we are not in the flesh and blood of this body doesn't mean that we no longer exist. At least that's what I believe." Smitty paused and looked at Carl sitting so innocently across from him in the diner booth.

"Have you ever seen a ghost, Carl?"

"No sir, I don't believe in no ghosts. Come on, really?"

Smitty fired back, "Well Carl, that is your decision to believe whatever you want, but I don't have any choice in the matter." Carl became even more curious now.

"What do you mean by that?"

"Carl, it all comes down to you having an open mind. People can't tell you what to believe. Like all things in life, you must be your own man and decide for yourself what is truth, and that applies to everything in life. When you get a bit older and have your own experiences, you'll see what I mean. But let's just say that…that maybe… I've seen some "things" and we'll leave it at that."

When they were finished with breakfast, Smitty left his usual $1.25 tip for the waitress and winked at her on the way out. She blushed and looked away in embarrassment. There was something that was unspoken between them. Carl failed to notice.

After they left the diner they headed back to Indian Neck to the barber shop for a haircut. As they entered the small shop, an old brass bell rang over head announcing their arrival. The air was filled with the scent of aftershave and talcum powder. Cigarette smoke hung in the air like a curtain. On the wall hung some old sports banners and two wood-framed mirrors that advertised the names of whiskey. There were the usual men's magazines on the table that Carl took note of: a Playboy and a Sports Illustrated swimsuit edition. He didn't quite know it yet, but he was soon to be very interested in those.

Smitty made introductions, "Chuck, you old son of a bitch, how are you?" The old man and the barber shook hands and exchanged insulting hellos before he introduced the boy.

"Who's this walking in your shadow, Smit? A hitchhiker or something?"

"This is my newfound grandson from New York City, just showed up yesterday. I'm keeping an eye on him for the summer while my daughter is taking some summer courses going for her masters degree you know," he said proudly.

Chuck, with his greased back hair and white barber's coat, turned to Carl. "Nice to meet you son... and what will it be for you two gentlemen today? I know you only have three hairs left Smitty, but I gotta charge you full price." It was hard for Carl to tell if Chuck was being insulting, sarcastic, or maybe attempting to be funny.

"High and tight for me and a crew cut for the boy. And don't over charge me this time."

It was obvious to the barber that the boy needed a good clean up, but he stayed polite, out of respect for his friend. Chuck resigned, bit his lip, not saying what was really on his mind after that. Sometimes all you need to do is look at a man's face to know what he's thinking. Today that was exactly what had happened when Chuck and Smitty locked eyes after the hair cutting was all finished. He simply accepted his dollar tip and promptly turned his back to them.

"Thanks for stopping by you guys," and then he started talking to his next customer.

While they were walking back to the truck, the old man turned to Carl.

"Hey, you look sharp, kid!" Carl suddenly felt embarrassed, not knowing how to respond to a basic compliment.

"After lunch we'll head over to Caldor and pick you up some more summer clothes. I see you didn't bring much of anything with you." Carl looked up at the old man and smiled like this was the best day of his whole life. So far there were pancakes, haircuts and new clothes. Carl wasn't accustomed to getting this much of anything since his dad had left town. He wasn't used to having someone's undivided attention. Back in New York when at home, he often sat alone in silence drawing his own comics, being mostly ignored by his mother who was always busy correcting her school papers.

3

The following day was a bit boring for Carl, as they mostly sat around the house watching the news and the baseball game into the afternoon. Smitty looked at Carl.

"Let's go for a ride," his grandfather said, noting Carl's boredom. "We gotta see my old friend from the service."

They hopped into the old Ford and drove slowly around the block. Carl looked up at Smitty as if to question, "Why so slow?" Smitty's good friend, Irv, was just one street over from his house from what Carl could tell. They passed an old guy out watering his flowers. Smitty held his arm out the truck window and stuck up his middle finger until the other old man recognized him and gave him the middle finger right back. They smiled at each other, knowing it was an inside joke.

"What cha' up to, asshole?" said the man watering his flowers in his thick Yankee accent when they got out of the truck.

"The usual, I'm here to drink all your beer."

"Again?" replied the old man. "Come grab a chair, you old son of a bitch." Smitty's friend, Irving, had failed to notice there was a young boy in tow and quickly apologized for his language once he saw him. Irv held out his hand to shake the boy's and said, "Nice to meet yah' kid. What's your name?"

Smitty interrupted. "This is my newly found grandson, Carl." Irv raised an eyebrow, as if to ask the most obvious question without actually saying it.

"Give me just a minute, Smit," said Irv.

"Hey kid, go just around back to where the garage is, in the back you'll find an old white fridge. Just pull the big chrome handle in the center of it. If it sticks a little, tug hard. There are Nestle Crunch bars in the freezer, help yourself. Oh and there are some sodas to the left of the beer, if you want one I think there's birch beer and crème flavor… just dig around, and you'll find them"

Irv and Smitty sat down and they both grabbed a Schlitz beer from the Igloo cooler, sitting on the front porch. Irv then looked to Smitty.

"Is this the kid your daughter had with that black guy down in the City?" Irv finally asked. Did she just dump him off on ya' or something?"

Only he didn't say black guy but something more derogatory instead, which offended his friend only momentarily. Smitty glanced at him, then looked away. Back in their "factory days," this was just normal everyday talk. Only this time it was about his family. The insult was much more personal, and the circumstances changed everything.

"Yes," replied Smitty. "That's the one. Careful how you talk about my grandson, Irv."

"Gotta hand it to ya' Smit. You got a big heart, my friend. I don't know what I would do if I was in your shoes, pal." This was all being said while he was trying to save face after the blunt insult to his old friend. Neither one looked at each other for a while and just sipped their cold beers until Carl came back around the corner with both an ice cream and a soda in hand.

"What flavor did ya' pick out, kid?" "Creme," Carl replied.

"Give it here, I'll open it for you." Irv paused for a moment. "So Carl, what are you after these days? Comic books, girls, models, cars?"

The boy just looked up at him and shrugged his shoulders not knowing quite what to say. He wasn't accustomed to this kind of sarcastic Yankee humor.

A moment or two passed as they all sat there quietly watching the traffic go by until Irv spoke again.

"Hey Carl, ya' know what? We should all go out fishing together on your grandfather's boat this weekend. What do ya' say? Have you ever been fishing?"

"No sir, I never have," the boy replied. His mother had always taught him to be polite when addressing adults, but his dad was indifferent. He instead had a permanent chip on his shoulder. Carl sat there and remembered how his dad wasn't very good at conversations with him, or anyone else for that matter. As a result, he was socially awkward. Irv got excited by Carl's answer.

"What? Really! You haven't been fishing before? Come on, you're pulling my leg, kid? Well, Smit, we gotta teach this here boy about fishing for some blues out in the Sound then. My friend, Johnny, said they're running right now."

"Yes, that sounds like a good idea. Sure we can do that. You bring the bait and the beer since this expedition was your idea."

Smitty was annoyed that Irv just invited himself, acting like he owned the boat or something. Irv shrugged at his friend's demand and then said, "Fine, I'll do that."

Carl had lost track of the conversation at this point and was day dreaming again about his absent father. Deep down inside he felt hurt and wondered if his dad's leaving was his fault somehow. There wasn't anyone he could really talk to about these feelings, outside of his own mother, but she was off taking summer classes, working towards her Masters Degree in Education. If she didn't get it, she would be stuck with her crappy union pay. For now their circumstances dictated that she grab the bull by the horns and make this happen for both of them. There was rent, food, clothes and utilities to pay. She was often heard saying, "The city ain't cheap." This all hung over his mom's head like a long shadow that spit out fervent ineptitudes.

The weekend eventually came around and they were going to go out on the Long Island Sound for some blue fish. "Remember it's fishing, not catching," the old man told Carl.

Like any good Yankee fisherman, Smitty even had a couple lobster pots that were home made. They were a bit rough looking, but they served their purpose. He referred to the lobsters as being "tasty sea cockroaches." The boat was an ivory white, fifteen-foot Boston Whaler with a 60 horse power outboard Evinrude motor on it. It was his true pride and joy. On the aft, its name was printed in royal blue letters. It both said and declared, "My Way." The name struck Carl as being kind of weird.

"Smitty, what does the name on your boat mean?"

The old man smiled, looking down at him with glee because of the poignant question. Standing there, holding his arthritic left hand, he gainfully cracked his old swollen knuckles. All the while he was thinking about how he should respond to the boy's question. Finally, after a few moments, he turned to the boy.

"Well Carl, the reason that it says "My Way," is as a man in this world, I have worked hard to earn my place within it. My life, you see, has had meaning, and that is important. Your life should have meaning too, Carl. And you should know that everything I have I've worked for. So, if you are in my house for example, things are "My Way." I worked for it. I paid for it. It's my rules. But it's also because it's important to realize what it is you're working towards in your life. There needs to be an objective, or rather, you have to have a reason for being. If you work hard, it's perfectly okay to be selfish. It's mine and nobody else's. Does that make sense to you Carl?"

Carl had a glazed-over look in his eyes, "Sure, I guess so," he replied back. Though he was now more interested in the fact that Smitty had just pulled a gun out from his front pocket and put it into the glove box of his prized boat.

"Smitty, what's that? Why you got a gun for fishing?"

"You're full of questions today, huh? I carry it for my personal protection, of course. A man has to keep safe out on the water."

"Protection from what?" he asked, as if there were something out there on the water that Carl needed to be afraid of.

Half jokingly Smitty said, "It's for the pirates, of course but not the kind you see in the movies. There has been a rash of thefts up and down the East Coast for these here Boston Whaler boats. Boats, just like mine, have gone missing all the way up past New Hampshire into Maine even. These boats were special because they were 'unsinkable' You could even cut them in half with a chain saw and they would still float. The boat has a solid foam core, just like the stuff coffee cups are made of. Oh, and that reminds me... this one time I caught some guys cutting the lines to my lobster pots and so I shot a hole clean through the bow of their boat. You wanna talk about scared? They turned white and got away from me right quick."

Smitty grabbed the gun, opened the cylinder and emptied out all five rounds of his .38 Special into his hand before putting the cold steal into Carl's young hand for a closer inspection. Very sternly Smitty said, "The first rule of gun safety is to always point it in a safe direction, as you never know if it is loaded or not! These things are not toys and are nothing like what's in your comic books, Carl."

"Where did you get it?" The gun was a very foreign object in his everyday world.

Smitty continued on by saying, "A friend of mine used to work over at the Charter Arms gun factory in the valley. I was able to get it at cost, thanks to him. This model is called "The Undercover." Guns are tools, just like a hammer, but they ain't no toys. If you see one laying around, you go tell an adult right away, okay? Am--I--clear--Carl?"

"Yes sir. Can I shoot your gun some time?"

"Maybe, we'll see." Just then, Irv showed up with the bait and beer in hand. This prompted Smitty to reload the gun and stow it back away for safe keeping.

After the three companions launched the boat that morning, and headed out into the waters of the Sound, both Smitty and Irv discussed politics for what seemed like hours. The exchange had its moments where it seemed like they were arguing. You might say it got a little heated at certain points.

This was to be an election year, and the election was only about four months away. The presidential race of '84 was to be the sitting president Ronald Reagan vs.

formcr vice president Walter Mondale. Both of the old men were staunch Republicans, but Smitty didn't agree on everything the party stood for as of late.

As they arrived at what they called their "secret magic fishing spot," they dropped a few pots over the side with foam buoys, which were painted both powder blue and yellow. Every lobsterman had his own unique colors so as to not get mixed up with another guy's pots. The only problem was that here in the Sound, theft of pots was common. If one guy had fished a certain spot long enough, he tended to think he owned it. It wasn't unheard of for fist fights to happen back at the docks over this, if it wasn't settled out at sea. For some guys, lobsters were their livelihood, and good money too, so they were able to pay their mortgage's by fishing these waters. "Don't ever mess with a man's paycheck, especially not that of a fisherman," said the old man to Carl.

Irv pulled out a small plastic container that carried the sand worms that they were to be using as bait that day. Each rod was rigged with two, #2 hooks and a lead weight tied to the end. These were used closer to shore for getting stripers. After that, they would switch locations and rigs and use a chrome plated lure with a three pronged treble hook for the blue fish. Smitty saw the chrome-plated lure, and his mind immediately went off to another place. The shiny reflective surface reminded him of the Foo-Fighter he had seen while he was in the Navy. Both Carl and Irv had taken notice of him zoning out. Irv yelled to him, "HELLO, where did you go?" Smitty shook his head and just ignored them. He went back about his business like nothing had happened.

Irv was explaining to Carl that with these shiny lures they would constantly be casting and reeling, over and over again, which bored Carl to death. When they finally hooked what was determined to be a nice blue fish, they yelled out "FISH ON!", then let Carl reel in the fish. Around noon time the sun came out, and it got really hot out on the waters despite there being a breeze. Smitty turned to Carl, "You wanna jump in and cool off kid? You can take a piss too."

"No... I don't know how to swim!"

"What? You don't know how to swim?"

"Yep, I can't swim...I just sink."

Smitty looked over to Irv, who was shaking his head in disbelief. Smitty then said, "Okay, we're gonna fix that right quick. Put on this here orange life-vest and cinch it real tight; loop it under your crotch so it's snug."

Carl reluctantly did as instructed, sensing what was to come. Irv winked at Smitty, then picked up Carl from behind and dropped him over the side into the cold waters of the Sound. At first, he protested and screamed. Once he realized that he wasn't drowning, but was instead floating, he quickly figured out how to doggy paddle his way back to the boat. He didn't talk to either one of them all the way back to the dock. Sitting and sulking in a hardened silence, he felt totally defeated. From now on he would be more careful in what he divulged to the two old men.

That evening they cooked dinner out in Smitty's back yard. He brought out a large pot for boiling the lobsters and a smaller one to be filled with corn oil, so they could fry the blue fish. Carl learned that blues were called a "same day fish." You had to eat them right away, as they didn't transport very well. Two of the neighbors, who were as old as Smitty, invited themselves over for dinner offering up a salad and some red potatoes in return. He seemed to bark out his orders, like he was the head chef at a fine restaurant. The woman from next door was always a "nosey busybody," Smitty would say.

Looking down her nose at them, she then inquired, "Smitty, who's the boy who has been staying with you? He a stray you picked up on the streets down in New Haven or something?"

Irritated, he turned a bit red, clenched his fists, looked her straight in the eyes and said, "He's my grandson, Carl, ya' got it?"

The old man got defensive and made it clear by his demeanor that the inquisition ended with just that one question. Sometimes a look can speak more than words can ever express, especially when you hit the right nerve, and hit a nerve she did.

That evening they all sat around the large wooden picnic table for hours talking about the upcoming election, with Reagan being favored to win. There was also talk of their time in the service and who caught the biggest fish during their outing.

Then there was Carl, who was still irritated about the whole swimming lesson and said very little throughout the meal. He did, however, take notice that Smitty had gotten mad at the lady next door. Not quite knowing what it was about, he assumed it was about him. Carl, who was mulatto, stuck out like a sore thumb standing next to his pale white English Catholic grandfather. But it didn't matter to the old man. To him, they were blood and like they say, "that runs deep."

4

It was a typical hot and humid fourth of July day, and the old man and the boy were out walking through downtown New Haven admiring all the collegiate architecture of Yale University. Smitty lectured the boy as they were walking.

"Carl, this school is the antithesis of the rich and poor. Behind these walls lies both great wealth and prestige. Outside of them, however, it's just everyone else. The difference between rich and poor here is so blatant and in your face. The school may be dressed up with its fancy buildings to create feelings of reverence and prosperity, but ya' wanna know what I think? I think the exact opposite is true. As a man, you can dress up like either a gentleman or a pauper, but the clothing doesn't make the man. A nice suit don't change that fact that you're a greedy pig either. Now Carl, I'm not spitting in the eye of education here, as it does have its place in the world, but mark my word, there will come a day when these institutions turn their backs on us tradesmen and the like."

"You know, those who are the real men here are the ones who work with their hands. As men, we are not all cut from the same cloth, but we are most certainly the fruit of the tree that we fall from. Some of us get lucky though, and are just born into the wealth, and some of us are destined to bust our humps and fight for every penny we ever get. Remember this Carl; you have to decide who you are going to be in this world, as the disparities and prejudices will come up against you and test your metal. They will look at you judgmentally because of your skin color and assume you are lesser than them. Therefore, you must be willing to work twice as hard as some other men who are of lesser merit. Carl, if you ever feel bad about your circumstances in life, I want you to hold onto that feeling, and never let it go. Use it as the fuel that inspires your passion to succeed! You are better than them!"

Just around the corner, both Carl and Smitty passed a few homeless men pandering for money. The smell of urine and old beer assaulted his nose. They were surrounded by the usual cardboard boxes, newspapers and empty single serving liquor bottles. One of them had on an old olive drab jacket from when he was in the service. Smitty could tell it was from Nam. He reached into his front pocket and pulled out a few singles and put them into the man's cup. The homeless man then replied, "God bless you friend, thanks so much!"

"No, thank you, brother, for your service!"

They rounded the next corner, and just before they approached the hot dog vendor, Carl asked, "Smitty, why did you give money to just that one man?"

The old man puffed up his chest and replied, "He was obviously a veteran. He served our country. It doesn't matter what he looked like to me, I gotta help a guy like that out when I can. He was a fellow soldier too, and I always help out a brother in need. That's kinda how me and Irv are for each other. Yes, I know, he has some issues with flashbacks from when he was in the service. There were times he'd be down at the VFW drinking his face off and I'd go pick him up, drag him out of there and sober him up again and again and again. Best thing you can do for a guy like that is to just let him talk it out. I would get him to start talking about things he saw and experienced, so it wasn't just all bottled up in his head. And I know, he's a bit salty around other people, but he's a factory guy just like me, not a lawyer or even something worse. We're all brothers, us veterans. We gotta watch each other's backs."

After eating their lunches, they headed over to the News Haven store to buy Carl some of his favorite comic books: X-Men, Hulk and G.I. JOE. As they were standing there in the confined space of the store on Chapel Street, Smitty looked over at Carl and winked and gave him a poke. Standing next to him was a man reading magazines, wearing sandwich bags on his hands.

Smitty being protective, said, "Let's get outta here Carl, now!"

Carl, not realizing what Smitty was driving at, looked up at the man with sandwich bag hands and locked eyes with him. Instinctively, he took a big side step away from the stranger. He stayed tight up to Smitty's side until they had left the store. It wasn't totally foreign for Carl to see these types of people since he was from the City. His mother would usually just grab him by the elbow and steer him in the other direction.

The pair left after they had made their purchase and headed back to Smitty's house on Branford Point. Their plan was to waste away the afternoon reading comics, watching the Tour de France on the television, and maybe cook some hot dogs on the grill. Smitty sometimes liked to quote Walt Whitman by saying "and we shall just loaf," which made Carl laugh.

As they rounded the corner to the old man's street, Smitty cursed out loud, which Carl was getting used to by now. He raced the old truck forward and drove up onto his front lawn. He then barked an order at Carl to "run next door and get Mrs. Carson, right away, just do it!" The old man quickly jumped out of the truck and ran across the street ignoring all of the on coming traffic. The old man was now a reflection of his younger glory days, running to snatch up the red-haired, 3-year-old girl who was left outside all alone in the neighboring driveway. He could see that the child was clearly in distress. Smitty did his best to console the child until Mrs. Carson made it over to Carl to assist. Smitty looked totally enraged.

"Let's head over to my house so I can call the police, Carl. That lady across the street is a no-good, God-damned drunk I tell ya'! I just knew something like this was going to happen sooner or later. I've been watching her for awhile now. Some people shouldn't breed."

About ten minutes later, a police cruiser arrived, followed shortly by an ambulance. All the neighbors were now watching the spectacle unfold. The officer who came to the scene was less than friendly to Smitty in his inquisition for the "facts."

The short-tempered officer said, "You know this kid?"

"Not really," Smitty replied. "I just live across the street. Most days I sit out on the front porch here and I see what's going on. The mother is a fucking drunk and just left the kid all by herself, out in this heat, all by herself, alone I tell ya'! What else do you wanna know?" Smitty was losing his patience with the officer and stood upright to enforce his point of measure.

"Are you trying to help or be some sort of prick?"

"Look mister, I just need to make sure no one else here was involved somehow. These type of child welfare cases can get tricky."

"Yeah, we're involved! We're good, honest, hard working people, buddy. We look out for one another in this neighborhood! Is that a crime? Usually you say "thanks" for that kinda thing or did I miss something here?"

"Calm down buddy, just gotta ask, that's all."

The whole "lost child" drama came to an abrupt end after thirty minutes or so. Smitty gave his name and number to the officer for any further questions. He ended the conversation by saying, "Here's my number in case you wanna ask me out on a date or something. Or maybe just call to break my balls some more."

Carl noticed how Smitty didn't seem to like cops. He didn't dare ask why.

Afterwards, the old man and the boy sat outside in silence for a longtime, drinking their sodas. Smitty was still trying to calm down for a long time after the whole episode. His temper could go from zero to ten quickly, and Carl was keeping an eye on him for that now too.

A while later an unmarked, black, police cruiser pulled up in front of the house. A nicely dressed man emerged from behind the tinted glass. He looked intimidating wearing mirrored sunglasses. Smitty hurried out and met him at the sidewalk. Carl just sat and watched with a bated curiosity. The two men stood there in the afternoon sun talking for nearly fifteen minutes. The man in the suit shook his head back and forth as to say "no" and then left abruptly. Smitty then came back to the house and walked past Carl, not saying a single word. Carl didn't dare ask what this second police inquiry was about. He came back out a few minutes later with a scotch in hand. Carl was too curious and asked,

"Smitty, who was that man you were talking to?"

"It was nobody Carl, forget that he was even here." In a low tone he said, "You get what I'm saying?" His demeanor was severe and a little threatening.

"Sure… I guess so…"

"Okay then, let's just sit here quietly for a while and watch the traffic go by, shall we?"

Carl, half whispering said, "Yeah, sure."

Later, both Carl and Smitty walked out to the Point with their lawn chairs and cooler. There they sat in silence watching the fireworks going off overhead. Around ten o'clock they headed back to the house, still not saying a word to each other. Carl stayed up late after brushing his teeth before bedtime and was drawing his comics like he normally did. Always generous to the boy, Smitty bought him an artist's notebook with an assortment of colored pencils. He occupied himself for hours on end drawing and making up stories. Most of them were what he had done that day. Some were inspired by what he heard from the old man too. Smitty, who was still a bit un-nerved was also awake and came in to check on Carl. Startling the boy, he said,

"Hey Carl, I wanna show you something. Follow me, kid."

Carl followed him down the hall, and they went into the third bedroom, which was now Smitty's library. He had an entire wall filled with books, some of which were on military history, fishing, woodworking and others that were the hard bound classics like Moby Dick and Gone With the Wind. These were similar to the ones that you might see at the public library. On the wall directly behind his desk, there were also some old family photos alongside some other pictures that were from his time in the Navy. At the far end of the room sat his Quaker-style desk made from solid oak. It was accompanied by two green leather wrapped Soto chairs. They were set out in front of the desk like some businessman might have done in a proper office building.

Only one wall in the study had wallpaper on it, which Carl found to be weird and out of place. It had a busy pattern with garden flowers on it, something like you might find on the wall of an old colonial inn.

Smitty told Carl to "have a seat" as he was pointing to one of the two chairs. Sitting there like the boss, he was looking down at Carl, paused, and lit his pipe. He looked important sitting behind his nice wooden desk, the boy thought. Carl reached for the bright yellow butterscotch candies on the desk, making himself feel more at home. After a moment or two had passed, Carl could see the look on Smitty's face change. The look became more discerning and almost severe. It was like he was preparing for something while studying Carl, as he sat there innocently eating his candy. After a few puffs from the pipe, he broke the silence and spoke. It was almost like he was preparing for confession at church.

"I need to tell you some things about my life Carl, and some are very complicated and hard to explain to someone your age. You see, sometimes the worst things about people are actually the best and the most interesting too. Every man's life is its own unique story. Like the books over there on the shelf. Some of these stories will get told, if they are lucky, but more often than not they die on the lips of the person who had lived them."

"Carl, I'm looking at you now and I see my legacy before me. I see it living on well past my years. If I'm being honest here, I have no qualms with the things I've had to do during my time in the service. I did what was asked of me, and I think I've earned my place in this world for doing that. Now… I need you to stick out your pinky finger, please." Smitty then leaned over the desk and locked pinkies with Carl.

"I need you to pinky-swear on your life, that you'll keep my secret until it's time for my story to be told." At first, the boy hesitated.

"Okay, sure I promise," he said, with some reservation in his voice.

Smitty then got up from his desk and went over to the one wall covered in wallpaper. He ran his hand down low against the wall until he felt a raised seam. It was a hidden seam, one which wasn't really visible to the naked eye from a distance. Once he came to the right spot, he pushed on it until a secret panel popped off.

Getting down on all fours, Smitty reached into the deep cavity in the wall, and pulled out a round, metal, potato chip container. It was brown and yellow with fancy print on it. Smitty brought the container over and placed it between him and Carl. Using his dirt filled nails, he pulled the lid off. Inside, Carl could see a yellow envelope labeled, "Blue Star, number 84." There were a couple of 8mm film rolls, a hand full of photos and a military surplus Remington 1911 with pearl pistol grips.

Smitty pulled the gun out first, and cleared it, dropping a round of .45 onto the carpeted floor, and then finally stuck it into his desk drawer. He locked it up for safe keeping. He only gave Carl a moment to look at the photos before quickly taking them back. Just having this contraband out in the open gave him anxiety. The photos had words written on the back which Carl didn't understand. One said Foo-Fighter, another said UFO, the last one was labeled black triangle. Smitty took the large tin and put it behind his desk before he started talking again.

Then, slowly lighting his pipe once more, Smitty started by saying,

"Carl, I want you to remember, this is TOP SECRET, and someday it will be your secret to hold onto. This secret is also my legacy, but for right now this story can't be told without people getting hurt, or maybe even killed. But, by the time I'm gone, it shouldn't really matter. Do you understand what I'm saying?"

Carl quietly nodded his head up and down, only he did not understand what he was agreeing to.

Smitty pulled open the center drawer of his desk and pulled out a tan colored piece of paper with Carl's name on it. He then explained to the boy that it was a bond worth $25,000.00 and that it would help put him through art-school, once he finishes high school. He repeated himself again, that the contents of the container will be your story to tell someday, hopefully through his artwork. Also, he said, "I think it will make a great comic book series," planting the seed of an idea into his head now.

Then Smitty just sat there, putting both hands squarely flat on the desktop in front of him.

"Trust me, this is a story that must be told someday, somehow or in some way. Carl, you must make that decision for yourself when the time is right. When you turn 25, I want you to call this phone number listed here in my green notebook. I always keep it here on the desktop, if you need to find it. You must tell the man that you are ordering "potato chips" and then give him your address. Got it? And one more thing, from now on, we will never speak of this ever again unless I'm giving you more instructions to carry out, okay?" Carl sat silently and nodded his head yes again. He was yet to realize the enormity of what was being asked of him.

That night, after Carl was fast asleep in his bed, he thought he heard Smitty's truck start and pull out of the driveway around 2:30.a.m, but wasn't sure. He just glanced at the clock on his nightstand and rolled over, continuing his sleep.

The next morning, Carl walked out to the living room only to find Smitty dead asleep with all his clothes still on, in his old armchair. Carl laughed to himself seeing him there with his socks and shoes still on. He let the old man sleep and went into the kitchen and put some strawberry Pop-Tarts into the toaster oven for breakfast.

Looking over at the back door, he noticed that Smitty's keys were still dangling from the door knob from last night. He quietly took them out and placed them into the wooden bowl on the kitchen table where the old man kept his wallet, checkbook, pocket knife and some loose change. Carl just sat there in silence, reading his comics. He had left his caretaker fast asleep until around 10a.m.

Breaking into the silence, the phone rang and woke the old man up. Carl answered, it was his mother on the line. She made her usual inquiries as to where they had been, how the fishing was, and if they had been to the movies lately. Carl replied flatly, with a basic yes or no, to most of her questions; he always felt that he was being interrogated by her somehow. The truth was that Carl's mom made every effort in their brief conversations to avoid having to talk about herself. Instead, she controlled their phone exchanges with a continuous barrage of questions. In other words, it was always a one-way conversation.

5

Sometimes in life, we aren't given the opportunity to grow up, but instead we are forced into the sudden maturity of adulthood by the wicked hand of trauma. Whatever prevailing circumstances the world gives us is that which we must take and make good. For Carl, it was like being a child who was thrown overboard into the dark ocean of humanity. Life it seems, only gives us two choices. You either sink or swim.

Later that day, Smitty, as a solitary figure, sat on Horseshoe Beach in the hot sand. He was looking down at Carl with the watchful eye of both the grandparent and a guard dog. The boy was now looked upon as both an investment and his personal legacy. For Carl, all of his reflections, thoughts and actions were to be studied by Smitty, the old man. He now held the boy in his hand like clay, ready to be molded. All his prospects in life must lead to only one outcome: telling the story of "THEM."

The end of July was quickly approaching. The summer Olympics were starting, and a hard drought had turned everyone's front lawns into a sea of tan and brown dust. People had given up on trying to water them. The beach was the only good place to be to get any relief from the searing heat.

Smitty was trapped in his thoughts. He sat in the sand reflecting, thinking on how only just a month ago he had taught the boy how to swim and plant tomatoes in the garden. They had planted his favorite beef-steak tomatoes and some frying peppers too. Part of the lesson he taught Carl was how to use the seaweed from the ocean as a fertilizer, cutting the heads off the fish, and then burying them underneath each plant in the Native American tradition. He patiently explained that the best fertilizers were from nature and not to use the chemical ones coming from factories. He continued in his reflection for some time until Carl, who was soaking wet, came up to join him on the beach towel.

The boy was standing over the old man dripping water on him until Smitty pushed him back. After drying off with an old faded bathroom towel, Smitty handed him a can of soda and his ham and cheese sandwich that he had made earlier. Reflecting, he laughed to himself, thinking how he had to stand next to the boy who was on a stool. There, in his kitchen, they had made sandwiches like it was a kind of factory assembly line. The old man and the boy, standing side by side. They were creating some good memories together this summer.

Smitty had jokingly said to the boy, "You'll never starve as long as you know how to make yourself a sandwich." He then went into a long monologue about how he always grew some of his own food in the garden and that Carl should try to be as self-reliant as possible in life. "You never know what tomorrow will bring," he often said.

Still lecturing Carl, he went on to say, "You can either be the guy buying the fish for money or the one catching them for free. Everything in life costs something, whether you like it or not. You need to teach yourself as many skills as you possibly can in life, Carl. Be a constant student. It's expensive to be stupid. If I had to pay some poor schmuck to come fix something every time that I had broken it, I'd be broke!" Carl looked away and rolled his eyes.

Smitty and the boy sat in silence as they ate their ham sandwiches on the beach, all while watching the small waves come sweeping in from the Sound. Carl was keeping an eye on some of the other kids he had been playing with in the ocean earlier on. They had been nice enough to share their floats with him. He was very pleased to know that in the innocence of play there were no prejudices here at the beach. It was something that was always in the back of his mind during social situations. It was something that a child should never have to worry about, but he often did.

After Carl finished his sandwich, he turned to the old man with a little hesitation.

"Smitty, I think… I think… I had a weird dream last night. It kind of scared me, too." He seemed embarrassed to have to admit this to him.

"What do you mean by 'kinda' scared you, Carl?"

"Well, I was in a big silver colored room, there was a large glass wall that I could see through, and there were these enormous bees behind the glass wall. I could see that there was a hole in the wall where the honeycomb was. The bees were so big, Smitty, like a small cat. But I stopped feeling scared when I looked into their big black eyes. Oh, and you wanna know what was really weird? I heard this loud metal machine noise and I felt like I was actually awake in the dream. Isn't that strange? What do you think it means?"

Flushed with fear, the old man looked away from the boy. His mind quickly started calculating the chances that this somehow might tie into his past with the Navy. The experience took place onboard the New Orleans vessel. He thought to himself, "No, it isn't possible! No, it can't be! How could they even have known that I had ever showed him that stuff? Maybe it was a freak coincidence and maybe I'm just being paranoid." His mind then jumped to the possibility of it being a screen memory, covering up the fact that a visitation had really happened. The E.T.'s would often show you one thing while an entirely different event unfolded before you. He knew extreme caution was needed now.

After a few moments, Smitty started talking to Carl but wouldn't look him in the eyes for fear of what he might find reflected in his young face.

He had a working base of knowledge on what he thought it really meant but didn't come out and directly say it to the boy. He just knew it was "THEM." Speaking in a low voice so that no one else could hear, he then asked,

"Carl, do you think it was like a movie you were watching?

"Yeah, I guess it kinda was…"

"And did you feel like you were watching yourself in the movie, like it all happened at the same time somehow?"

"Yes, I was there, and I was watching it happen at the same time, Smitty. How did you know that? Did it happen to you?"

"Yes, I've had such dreams too, Carl."

Carl sounded surprised that the old man knew what he was talking about but wasn't quite sure why. His head was stirring with so many questions that his young mind didn't know how to articulate, at least not just yet. However, in that moment all he could think about were those large black eyes that the bees had. The connection with them had stirred something inside. Thoughts within thoughts, like wheels with wheels turning. A mind getting ready to expand.

Still concerned, Smitty asked Carl to draw some pictures of "THEM," later on that night. He threw out the idea of making it into a comic book story, "So you won't forget it," he said with a wink. Carl was oblivious to his underlying motive. The old man acting like a hidden architect for the boys future.

The next morning when Carl woke up, he had a bloody nose (a tell-tale sign of an abduction for a child), and he instinctively went to Smitty for help. The old man, not knowing why, had the hair on the back of his neck standing up when he set his eyes upon the boy's bloody face. A blanket of silent guilt fell over him. He took Carl to the bathroom, washed his face off, and stuck some tissue paper up his nose. Then he asked his permission to examine the fronts and backs of his legs to see if there were any other obvious signs from "THEM." He did it under the guise of making sure he wasn't cut, or something else.

There were two parallel indentation lines running across each of his shins. Feeling concerned, the old man then asked,

"Carl, did you run into something when you were playing outside yesterday?"

"No, I don't think so. Why?"

"Oh... no reason, I just wanted to make sure you weren't hurt or anything, that's all."

Smitty quickly changed the subject to pancakes after a brief examination of the boy's legs. Intentionally, he had completely distracted Carl again by asking him if he wanted to go out for breakfast at Cody's, knowing he would be totally thrilled and forget the matter. Smitty quickly learned, as a new grandparent, how easy it was to make a young boy happy by bribing him with food. It was the simple things that meant the most to the boy.

Later that afternoon, both Carl and Smitty were hiking through the woods out at Gillette Castle again. This somewhat hidden stretch of woods had become one of Carl's favorite parks to visit. As they walked, Smitty was telling him the story of William Gillette, about how he was a famous actor and playwright. He was a big fan of his role that he had played as Sherlock Holmes, too.

The park was a nice sized parcel of forest to get lost in, stretching out over 122 acres of pristine forest. The park land also overlooked the beautiful Connecticut River Valley. Sometimes they would stop and sit on the edge of a cliff, like a sort of look out. There were areas of exposed grey granite jutting out with small pockets of quartz crystal veins in them. Smitty would sit and smoke his pipe while Carl would keep a lookout for the paddle boats going up and down the river. He would imagine the types of people who were lucky enough to get to ride on such boats.

Breaking in on their silence, Smitty sang a song from his Navy days.

"I knew a lad who went to sea and left the shore behind him...

I knew him well, that lad was me...

And now I cannot find him...

That lad was me..."

After he finished singing, Smitty then tapped out his pipe on the craggy rock face. Smitty told Carl about a toy store called Amato's over in Middletown. It wasn't too far from the castle. He used to take his mother there when she was a young girl. She had liked to buy furniture for her dollhouse, he explained. They had board games, paint supplies, model planes, and train sets too. Carl was excited with the prospect of getting more art supplies and maybe some paints with which to work. Smitty was just secretly keeping the young boy's mind busy and distracted with things to do, other than talking about "THEM."

Later that evening, both the old man and the boy sat in his study after dinner. They now had a routine, like an old married couple would. Smitty was writing his notes in his notebook about their day together, and Carl was working on painting his dream from the other night. The old man looked over and was surprised at what he saw on Carl's paper. As he studied it, he was growing more and more concerned as to where a child of his age would come up with such a drawing.

Smitty spoke softly to Carl and asked, "What exactly are you painting there, Carl? I see you've filled up a few pages now. Are they all one theme?"

"Yes, they are all one big picture that goes together like a puzzle."

"Have you ever painted before?"

"No... not really. I never had a paint set like this one before, just crayons and colored pencils. I really like this paint, Smitty, thanks." Carl looked up at the old man with a gracious smile, paused and then went back to his painting. Smitty was amazed, not realizing such ideas could come from such a young mind.

"Say Carl, please push them together so I can have a better look at them." The boy complied with the request and pushed them all together, so the four pages created one complete canvas. Smitty wasn't quite sure what he was looking at, but there were some obvious elements:

like stars, clouds, outer space and some sort of ancient building structure with symbols on it.

"Tell me what the story is supposed to be, Carl."

"This is from my dream, you see. There was an angel in this big open hall, but it wasn't a church. The white angel showed me how big the universe was and that we all have a soul, which is part of God. The angel was sad though, as there were no more souls left there in this hall to come back to Earth." Smitty's jaw dropped, he was that dumbfounded.

"Who told you this story? Was it in a bible study class or something?"

"Nope, it was in my dream, Smitty. I talked to the white angel."

Getting even more curious now, the old man asked, "Did you ever try and read any of the Bible before, Carl?

"No sir, no. I don't go to church, don't like that kinda stuff."

The old man wasn't quite sure what to make of this, but recorded it into his notebook so that he was keeping track of all their conversations. He knew the boy didn't understand most of what he had just said, so he made a detailed record of it for him, as a future reference. He realized then and there that this would be an important story for him to look back on one day.

"Carl, come sit in this chair for a minute, will ya'?"

"Yeah, sure, okay." Carl seemed annoyed to be interrupted. He always had to finish whatever he started before doing anything else. He sat down in one of the green leather Soto chairs facing the desk. On the desk was a large jar of brass buttons which always caught his eye. Carl was curious about the buttons, wondering where they had all come from and why Smitty was collecting them. Smitty then grabbed the jar and centered it on the desk in front of Carl. Then he spoke while holding his pipe in his left hand.

"You see these buttons, Carl? I've been collecting old military buttons for some time now. Anytime I go to a flea market, I buy them and add them to my jar. There are buttons from the Marines, Air Force and the Army. Each of these buttons is like their own individual person. I want you to imagine that you are a button in the very center of the jar."

Carl looked into the jar and squinted to see, imagining himself in there.

"You are the center button, and all the other buttons around you is everyone else. The glass jar is God, the creator. Now you can't see God, but he is there holding everyone together. The only proof that we have of God is that we are all being held together in this universe of ours. There is a thing called faith, Carl. Your faith is in knowing that God is there. The glass jar is like God's hands holding us all together. You can't see God, but your faith tells you that it in fact is. Does that make sense to you?"

"Yeah, I guess so. Will I ever get to see God, Smitty?"

"Yes, when you die, you leave the jar and go back to God." Carl smiled at the old man, then hopped off the chair and went back to his painting. He had heard the words, but their gravity were not yet realized.

6

Two weeks later, the old man and the boy were into the month of August. The summer drought was still holding tight, and the heat was well into the upper 90's now. The summer had become more about staying cool and enjoying things like swimming and eating ice cream during their hot afternoons together. Whenever Carl heard the ice cream truck, he ran to the old man and held his hand out. He rarely said no. The truck always came around 6p.m. too.

Here in Connecticut, the corn was now in season, the tomatoes were ripe and the dark green cucumbers were ready to be picked and sliced. The Atlantic red lobsters were easy to catch out in the Sound and if you were lucky, maybe catch some flounder too. During the height of summer, it was time to reap the rewards of what had been sown.

On one humid August night when there was nothing on TV, Smitty had sent Carl to go sleep in his bedroom. The boy put a blanket on the old man's bedroom floor, where the only air conditioner in the whole house was located. Smitty stayed up late smoking his pipe and writing his notes in his journal. His plan was that he would have them sent off to Carl after his passing. The harsh reality was that when you reach a certain point in your life, every day was a blessing. The old man now had this perspective on a lot of things, especially when it came to Carl. The boy had to know what was going on in his mind. This was tending to the seed that he had planted there about "THEM."

Whether or not this was subconscious or intentional was up for debate. He felt pushed to do this somehow, by an unseen force. An urge in his mind that couldn't be explained.

It was around 11p.m. and Smitty was still up late, working in his study, smoking and drinking whiskey on ice. He enjoyed his time alone and had forgotten how much he enjoyed his own company now that Carl was in his life. After he finished writing, he wandered over to his bookcase looking for something interesting to read. He had a small hand bound book called, "The Thinking Stones." It was given to him by a friend a long time ago. There was no publisher or author listed on this book, which made it a bibliographic oddity. One could say it was a very small hand-made publication; this is what made it so appealing to him. There he sat, reading into the early hours, simply enjoying his alone time.

The Thinking Stones: *It was the stones that brought man into the modern age of all things, and of that which he was able to create. The stones are said to have been here since the beginning of all things, in the known universe. The stones were estimated to each be 10 meters tall and 82 tons in weight. If a man were to find them, and actually have been able to stand between them, he would see one of three things: the future of all men, the past of all men, or possibly his own death, if he stood there too long.*

A man, who was said to have wandered the empty desert, had discovered them. The Thinking Stones had told the Desert Man that they had been there long enough to see the birth of the known universe. They had also been on our planet long enough to have been in the jungle, the grassy plains, and then finally, the hot desert before disappearing back into the Void.

The Desert Man was thought to be a time traveler, the one who came from in between the two stones. No one could be sure though, as the story had been retold so many times. He wore a dark black cotton tunic that covered his body from head to toe, so that you could only see his eyes. And his eyes were said to be the color of icy blue steel. One would have to look away if they stared into them too long.

The story handed down was this:

The Desert Man visited each of the first five tribes that had set foot upon the earth. He knew each of their languages but never spoke a word. Instead, he conversed with you through your mind. For each tribe, he gave a different gift.

The first received the knowledge of forging metals, the second tribe the gift of writing, the third tribe the knowledge of how the heavens moved, the fourth tribe the knowledge of making medicine, and the last tribe, most importantly, the history of the known universe. It was the story of the "Great Singularity."

He told each tribe the story of the Thinking Stones as well. They all needed to know that there were things in the known universe that could not be understood, no matter how much wisdom they obtained. The stones also gave a warning to tell about the year 2035. They showed him in his mind's eye that there would be eight inches of sea water rise over the lands and that enormous wildfires would destroy many of the great cities built by the hands of their future brothers and sisters.

-The End

Smitty would periodically sit and read this short story from time to time. It reminded him that there were indeed things that he could not understand in this universe. He had seen the UFOs and some other unexplainable phenomenon while he was in the service. Most of the observed phenomenon was classified above Top Secret and not even his best friend, Irv, knew about these things. This is both how and why he put so much stock into the boy and his future education. He could tell the story through him, without any of the legal repercussions after he was dead. Again, he thought to himself, "If I go and take the big dirt nap, I don't want this information to die with me." Slowly, he lifted the pipe to his lips and took another puff before finally retiring to his recliner. The smell of his cherry tobacco floated into the late night air, and a quarter dropped from the Void and hit the floor next to him. He looked over and smiled at the centennial twenty-five cent piece laying there beside him. This was confirmation from the Universe that he was doing the right thing.

7

A few days later, both the old man and the boy headed out to the Long Island Sound for yet another fishing trip. It was a Tuesday, another day that ended in the letter Y. The tides were agreeable, and the waters promised to be calm. "Pretty as a picture," Smitty would say, in his old Yankee accent.

Like a well-oiled machine, they woke up at 4:30a.m., got dressed, made breakfast, and then started their assembly line for making the ham and cheese sandwiches. Extra mustard for Carl and don't forget the State-Line potato chips. It was as if there were a mental checklist and they both systematically went though, checking off each and every item. Smitty would always say on the mornings that they went fishing,

"Okay, up and at em.' We have to shit, shave and shower! Get a move on kid!"

On the way to the dock they gassed up the Whaler at the local Exxon station and picked up some coffee and donuts. Carl had even persuaded the old man into buying him a comic book for the boat ride. This day, had the feeling of having a certain ease to it. This day felt very natural too, as if it had already happened somehow. Maybe the universe had purposely lined up all the ducks in a row, so that nothing could go wrong, however, this wasn't to be.

Two hours later, they arrived at the "magic spot" and decided to let the boat drift for a while as they set up their rigs before casting out. Carl had spotted a hand full of seagulls out on the water and pointed them out to Smitty, knowing it was a sign of life below the surface. Smitty smiled at him and patted him on the head, acknowledging how well he had trained the boy. They both took a minute to study the spot until the moment got old. Just a few moments later, a humpback whale broke the surface and made a huge splash, scaring the wits out of Carl. Smitty told him how rare it was to see a whale like that in the Sound. It was indeed a very good omen for them and he went on to tell Carl about how the Montaukett Tribe of Long Island had taught the first European settlers how to hunt whales in the Atlantic, and also how to use the whale oil for their lamps. Smitty loved talking history, especially early naval history. Carl just rolled his eyes at him when he'd go off on a tangent like this one.

Around 11:30a.m., Carl asked Smitty about having lunch early and he happily agreed to the idea. They left their poles for the time being hanging over the side, dangling the shiny chrome lures into the dark ocean waters while they ate.

The old man and the boy sat in silence for a good ten or fifteen minutes before Carl said,

"Hey Smitty! Look at that big cloud coming over us. Look, look, look! Isn't that weird? It's like a big circle." Smitty then got the full body chills.

The old man took pause, as there hadn't been a single cloud in the sky just five minutes earlier. He then got another cold chill that ran up the back of his neck, not immediately realizing that he had this same type of feeling once before. He slowly remembered that it was back when he was in the service. It was while he was assigned to the New Orleans, which sailed out of the Brooklyn Naval Yard.

He eventually replied, "Yeah, I see it Carl. That's certainly a strange sight, kiddo."

Just then, it drifted even closer as if under some sort of conscious control. They just sat there eating their sandwiches, watching and waiting for it to pass them by. Only it didn't pass; the cloud paused and hovered overhead like a canopy, blocking out the afternoon sun. The boat was now darkened by its shadow. Carl then looked up.

"Hey Smitty, look there! Now it's like there's a black triangle inside the cloud! Dang, that's wicked!" Then........the world went silent. Time had stopped.

Two and a half hours later, both Smitty and the boy were cruising back to the boat launch as if they were in some sort of mindless daze. They didn't say a single word to one another. The old man, slowly coming to, looked over at the boy and noticed that blood was running out of his nose, and he quickly snapped out of the daze. Abruptly, he pulled the throttle back, slowing down, so the boat came to a crawl. Looking down at his wristwatch, it now said two o'clock. Turning back, he looked around as if he were missing something. He looked down at his wrist watch again and realized, a little over two hours had passed. This was strange since it felt like no time had passed at all. Time was missing! This was like a reverse deja vu. He then grabbed a handful of napkins and handed them to Carl.

"Here kid, wipe your face your nose is bleeding again."

Carl hadn't even realized that his nose was bleeding. He looked down at the white square of cotton and then back to Smitty. He unexpectedly began to cry, only he didn't know why he was crying. A shock ran through him that was simply unexplainable. Carl then headed for the starboard side of the boat, and grabbed the railing with both hands. With a strong thrust he then projectile vomited the entire contents of his stomach in one swift burst. Smitty grabbed him a soda from the cooler chest and handed it to him.

"Here, drink this, Carl. A Coke will make you feel better. It settles the stomach."

Smitty suspected what had just occurred, but tried to play the situation down, so not to excite the boy. He heard of these types of stories from a couple of his books he had read by Jacques Vellee on alien abductions. Smitty was now very frightened. Visions of short men with dolphin colored skin swirled in his mind. He thought of grabbing his gun, but it was now after the fact. No bullet could save him. Quickly trying to change focus he said,

"You probably got too much sun Carl, and maybe some sea sickness, too. That happens to the best of us. It happened to me back in the Navy a few times, on rough seas. We'd been caught up in a Nor'easter, thought I was going down with the ship."

Feeling nervous, he kept talking to Carl non stop for the next half hour in hopes of distracting his mind somehow. He told Carl corny jokes from when he was a kid, stories about the Navy, and even about helping Irv one time when he got into a bar fight. He just went on and on and on until he had distracted the boy's mind enough to where he forgot what might have just happened. But deep inside, Carl knew.

Driving the boat, the old man's thoughts again started to drift back to his Navy days, and the memories all came flooding back in, seemingly with purpose. Stress was the trigger. A cold sweat was forming over his brow now. He started gripping the steering wheel even harder. Anxious, he reached into his pocket for a cigarette.

Turning his back to the wind, he clicked open the chrome plated Zippo. This too was a reminder from the Navy. The past was inescapable.

"Just stay focused," he thought to himself. "It will be okay… or will it?"

Back in the Navy, Smitty was on a cruiser that sailed out of the Brooklyn Naval Yard, just across from Manhattan sky line. The ship had what was considered to be a "secret and experimental" radar system onboard that used Surface Barrier Transistors. The New Orleans had been built with both aluminum and copper interwoven into the cabins of the upper decks. The vessel was painted matte gray all around, so no one could tell that she was different from any other vessels.

While Smitty was assigned to the cruiser, he was tasked to be a Boiler Tender, which also taught him the trade of plumbing. It was similar to what he was doing at the old paper mill. On the ship, however, he heard things from time to time, things that just didn't make any sense. The men would talk about seeing things, like strange apparitions. Logically he figured that this was a new boat, and no sailors had died on her yet. So what were the apparitions, if not ghosts?

On alternating days, at around 3a.m., the ship would power up the integral radar system, and all the men that weren't working their active controls were assigned to stand by at their designated stations. Only they had to be standing on a one-inch thick rubber mat. Smitty always thought this was queer since he didn't handle any electrical work in his area. A buzzer would sound, the lights would dim, and sometimes guys reported being able to taste the fillings in their teeth while the radar was powered up and in full use. If you were to look out of the porthole window, you might see a blue haze surrounding the whole vessel during such operations.

On one occasion, Rogers, who was Smitty's bunk mate, came into his work area and quickly shut the door behind him. He waited a few seconds to see if someone had followed him there. Once the coast was clear, Rogers hurried over to Smitty. He looked desperate, even scared.

"Here, buddy. Stash this folder in your toolbox for me, will you? Don't ask any questions, it's private stuff. Don't tell no one! I'll buy you a carton of smokes once we're back on shore. Oh, and one more thing; I was never here. Got it?" His eyes now started to look mean and almost threatening as he said this to Smitty.

Smitty, feeling pressured by his friend said, "Um, okay, sure thing. This is really fucking weird though. If I get in some kinda shit for this, I'm gonna kick your ass, you know?" He stood before Rogers cracking his knuckles, exercising his point. The sailor then took a step backwards, towards the door. Holding his hands in the air, he said,

"Trust me, it's nothing. Just remember to take your tools with you when you leave the boat; no one will say a thing." Smitty conceded by saying, "Fine…but you owe me!"

After Rogers left the furnace area, the lights dimmed one more time. Smitty was then lost in his own thoughts, worrying about what might be in the envelope. Standing at his work bench, he lit up a cigarette and took a long deep drag. His mind was lost in thought, thinking about his girlfriend, and buying a house back in Connecticut one day with the money that he had saved up from the service. He was the type of guy who was tight with his money and didn't believe in blowing it when he was on shore leave.

He stood there for a while still thinking, until out of the corner of his eye, he saw something move in the darkest reach of his workshop. Slowly, he dropped his hand from his lips and turned around to look. The temperature of the workshop had dropped by almost ten degrees. Instinctively his hand reached out for the biggest crescent wrench on his work bench. He saw something which had been hunched over in the corner moving towards him. It appeared to be a small, thin, greyish looking humanoid. Its skin was like that of a dolphin. It also appeared to have no definable sex either. The Grey had large dark eyes that terrified him to the core. They locked eyes with one another, and he stood there frozen still. He couldn't talk or scream for help. It was like something had taken control of his physical being. It then spoke to him without moving its lips. Smitty could hear it loudly and clearly in his mind.

"We who know, now know who you are. We are who we say we are. We are the Watchers." Rapid moving pictures flashed through his mind of all the aliens' activities here on Earth. It showed him their history too, and how they were using human DNA to save their own race. It emphasized, "You need to tell the story. Nothing else matters. You'll know when the time is right and who to tell. Nothing else matters. It's so this doesn't happen to your race, too."

Then it just fazed out like a shadow being hit by the sunlight and disappeared back into the corner. Alarmed, Smitty then ran to the head and puked for the next five minutes there after. Another sailor who came in to take a piss stopped and said, "Seasick, huh, buddy? Or you been drinken on duty?" He looked at the man and gave him the finger until he gave up and walked out of the head.

Looking up at the mirror, with a dazed look on his face, Smitty just stood there in a cold sweat, and he turned and puked some more.

For many weeks after the encounter with the Grey, Smitty hardly said a word to his crew mates, unless they had pressed him for conversation. He was lost, vacant, absent and cold. So many foreign thoughts had entered his mind. He was now seeing pictures of other worldly places too. Sleep was to become only a word in his vocabulary, since it was now impossible to do so. Day to day, he lived on both coffee and nicotine, as he was too afraid to close his eyes while laying in his rack at night. He had read every magazine and book that his bunkmates had brought onboard too. Time would pass like the sands sifting through an hour-glass. After his tour of duty was up, he told some of his mates that he would never re-up, as they like to say in the service. His plans to make a career of the Navy had ended here.

8

The day after the missing time event, Smitty was once again sitting back at his desk, staring down at a blank page, trying to make accurate notes about what had just happened the day before. He sat there and thought to himself, "I didn't just imagine all this, did I? No… no… I think it really happened, but what exactly happened? Was it "THEM," the Watchers? They're on to me, of that I am sure. Carl has had the dreams too; just like I did after my encounter. But it doesn't make any sense, and again, why me? How do they know?" And it was in these thoughts that Smitty finally realized that there was no lock or door to keep this phenomenon out of his life. Nowhere was safe.

Dark thoughts about his past were now at the forefront of his mind. A haunting memory of "THEM." He kept stopping and starting while writing his notes, all the while watching Carl sitting there on the floor, drawing out his fantasy comics. He saw how methodical the boy was when he sat and drew such pictures. It looked to be almost like some sort of meditation or altered state of being. The boy was entranced.

Slowly rising up from behind his desk, Smitty walked over to where his record player was and dropped the needle down onto the spinning vinyl. The record was by David Brubeck, who was one of his favorite jazz musicians, ever since way back when. The beat was obvious and intentionally written in 5/4 timing. There was the unmistakable piano tempo, with its two long beats, then followed by two short beats. Smitty remarked to Carl that this was one of his favorite tunes of all time. It was called, "Take Five." Carl looked up at him and smiled, and then went back to his drawing without saying a word. He then tapped his foot, keeping time with the music while laying on the floor drawing.

Smitty went back to his desk once more and sat down, grabbed his pipe, lit it, and took a few short puffs. He watched as the smoke hung motionless in circles before the old double hung windows. The afternoon light appeared to be infrared. A heavy mood hung over the room.

Refocusing his attention, he turned back to his writing journal. Realizing he had lost his train of thought, he blindly reached for his pen, knocking it onto the floor. "Oh shit," he thought. Getting down on all fours he couldn't find the pen. He then recruited Carl for help in the searching.

"Hey kid, come over here and help the old man find his pen, will ya'?" Carl scooted over to the desk on his hands and knees. Looking around he declared, "I don't see it anywhere, Smitty. It's gone, like magic, poof. Maybe it's like the reverse of the centennial quarters dropping out of nowhere, huh?" Smitty looked puzzled. He knew the boy was right.

"Yeah, something like that, I suppose."

In the days that followed, Carl repeatedly had bad dreams. He would wake up in tears and then go to Smitty in the dark of night, waking him up and asking to sleep in his bed. Carl was acting as if the old man could somehow protect him from these horrible visions, the one's haunting him at night. What Carl didn't know, and the old man had failed to explain, was that these were more than just dreams. They were in fact flashbacks and maybe post-traumatic stress disorder from the boat event.

Carl was slowly starting to remember the ugly bits and pieces of his alien abduction, remembering the fateful fishing trip. An eleven year-old boy has no vocabulary for these type of things, and the old man was too frightened to explain them to him. The truth laid off in a distant point in time for Carl. This was like a ball of knotted twine that would take years to unwind.

After some time had passed, Smitty finally worked up the nerve and sat the boy down in his study for a talk. He began by asking him about his dreams. He'd wanted to know about all the nuances of them, and maybe find out if there was a recurring pattern.

Smitty was sitting there on the edge of his oak desk like a detective while Carl sat on the floor looking up to him. Subconsciously, he was exerting his authority over the young boy and the whole of the situation as well. It was the old man's ego that would be the first thing to break, however, as he was very stressed.

"Carl, I want to know more about these "dreams" you've been having. I realize that you've come into my room at night totally scared, and I get it. Maybe if I know some more details, we can work together to fix this somehow." Seeming official, the old man had a pencil and notebook in hand. He took on the air of both a guardian and psychologist.

"First, I want to know how often you are having these dreams, and who or what is in them? When did they all start for you? Do you think we can work on that together?"

Carl felt trapped and slowly replied, "Sure, I guess so." Carl unexpectedly turned the inquiry back on the old man. "Why do you think I have these bad dreams, Smitty?"

"Well, I think you may have seen something that your mind couldn't explain. It's called the supernatural. So, maybe it's like seeing a ghost and getting scared and then thinking about it too much afterwards. It sort of carries on and on until it gives you a bad dream. I'm going to keep some notes on them for you, alright? If there are any dreams you want to share with me, you just go right ahead and say so, Carl."

Carl told the old man all about his dreams. "In the first one, I was crawling through a long grey tunnel, and then I came into a dimly-lit room. I kept crawling on the floor until I could see downwards. There was a bright green baseball field far below me. From way up high, I could see the people playing ball. Then, I felt like I was being watched, so I looked up. Across from me, was some kind of skinny grey man who was all smooth skinned and he had these big black bug eyes!" Carl was now talking really loudly, and Smitty told him to lower his voice. He could see that the boy was getting worked up.

"The second one, well it wasn't a dream, but it scared me. I woke up in bed naked one morning, and I was just sitting up with my knees to my chest. It was like I was hiding from something, but I didn't know what it was. It was weird and out of place. I felt like I just got back from somewhere too."

"Oh, and I had already told you about the third dream, the one with the bees in it. You remember?" "Yes," the old man replied. "The one's with big black eyes behind the glass wall."

"In the fourth dream, I ran out onto the lawn where we all play soccer and locked arms with four other kids. I think they were about the same age as me. Then a bright blue light came down and sucked us up into a spaceship. While I was in the light beam, it felt like I was being held under water. Next, I was in a classroom with a white chalk board that had writing on it. Up on top of it was a collection of different types of soda cans. Some of those sodas had funny writing on them too. On the board was a fancy painting of a buffalo; it was like the one I had seen at the museum. And then I was shown another photo of a buffalo, but it was like a solid black-stamped outline of one. Yes, it was like a symbol of a buffalo. I suppose it was to mean the same thing. Then I just woke up. I really felt happy after that dream. It was a good one... this time."

"In the fifth dream, I was in a round room again. But this time, I was hanging in the air. I was naked. An ugly, brown alien creature was talking to me. He wanted to heal me and said I was sick. It then took a long metal tool and stuck it down my throat and pulled out this black blob. It was nasty! I was crying and screaming, but it didn't care. After that, it told me it was time to go home, all better now. When I woke up my stomach and mouth hurt bad, I could still taste the metal."

"That was the morning when you just wanted to stay in bed, right?"

Carl was surprised the old man knew and said, "yes."

Smitty was in deep thought, he then drew in a slow and steady breath. Clearly he had gotten so much more than he could assimilate. At least not in this moment.

He scribbled away on his note pad while Carl just stared up at him, suspended, waiting for an answer or possible explanation. He would have to tread lightly and act as if these were really just dreams. Even though he knew the truth, and the truth was ugly.

He thought to himself, "There's no way I can tell him right now, that this "thing" is really real. He's only eleven years old, for Christ's sake." It wasn't in his nature to lie, but he felt, in this moment, it would be necessary, to preserve Carl's innocence. After all, this was most likely in connection to his past. Yes, this "thing" was his legacy. So, he just sat there, thinking to himself, playing a mental game of tug-of-war within himself until he resolved to answer. Smitty then broke the acrid silence.

"Well… you see… when I was back in the Navy, I too saw some really weird stuff, Carl. It was Top Secret kinda stuff, and I'm not supposed to talk about it. No, not even now. So, you see, you're not alone, and other people have had these type of experiences, too. We'll keep notes on them for safe keeping, okay?" Carl felt cheated and didn't reply. He clearly saw that the old man was avaiding the real question.

Smitty, feeling the stress, then started to think to himself about the "alien being" he had seen onboard the New Orleans, the one that simply vanished in front of his very eyes. A cold sweat broke out on his forehead until the tension finally broke him. Nervously, he spoke once more but only this time in a voice of cowardice.

"Hey, let's go take a ride over to Irv's house and steal his soda, shall we? And maybe we can talk again later tonight, all right?" Carl quietly conceded.

"Sure, okay. Hope he still has that same crème soda. Oh, and can I have his ice cream again, too?"

"Yes of course, sure thing, kid."

For the moment, Smitty had chosen the path of avoidance. He didn't want to throw anything else on the boy's young shoulders right now. Especially since next week he was going back to the city, and the boy really didn't want to leave for New York, not just yet.

Ten minutes later, they were in the truck, sitting shoulder-to-shoulder, on their way over to Irv's. The old Ford was puddling along at twenty-five miles an hour. Carl would often say to Smitty that he drove like an old grandpa. Smitty would tell him that is because he was, and he wanted to make sure Carl was always safe. In the truck, the old man watched him out of the corner of his eye. He could see the tension in the young boy's eyes. He hoped and he prayed that the boy would make it. He had to tell the story. Again he selfishly thought that was all that mattered. "They" told him it must be!

Both Carl and Smitty pulled up to his old friend's front yard. In his usual fashion, Smitty gave Irv the middle finger as they pulled up. Irv was out in front putting a new coat of white paint on his small beach cottage. Smitty had inadvertently driven over the curb, then the sidewalk and some of the lawn, too. Irv got pissed and yelled at him.

"Time to hand in your fucking license old man! You blind or something?" Smitty looked at him as he slammed the truck door.

"You can bite me, Mister! Hey, Carl, go down back and grab yourself a soda and ice cream, and get a beer for me too."

Irv, taking notice said, "So what's eating at you, huh? I can see it in your face, old friend. Got some bathroom trouble or something? Maybe go eat some prunes," he said jokingly.

"No, no, it's nothing like that. It's nothing that I can't handle."

"Oh, there you go again, the big bad captain of secrets."

"Yep, that's me all right." Changing the subject Irv asked,

"How long is the kid staying for anyway? The summer is almost over, and he probably has school next week, right?"

"Yeah, my favorite daughter should be here by either Thursday or Friday to pick him up. At least she sounded a little happier when I talked to her last. I know she's had a handful of problems as of late. I told you all about her long-time boyfriend running out on her. Once upon a time, I told her that I didn't like his kind, and she stopped talking to me after that. Anyway, I hope it's all sorted out by now, at least for Carl's sake. His dad's a sorry excuse of a man for skipping out on him! If it were up to me, I would just have him keep staying with me. It's better than living alone, right?"

With some charity in his voice, Irv replied, "We're just a couple of old farts, huh?" And then Irv let out a raspy laugh that was choked back by a thick mucus. He grabbed his handkerchief and coughed some more. Looking down, he checked if there was any blood on it this time. Decades of smoking had finally caught up to him. The COPD was starving him of oxygen too. He figured it was too late to care, and it wouldn't make any difference if the "Big C" caught up to him. The black death was watching and waiting for him on the other side.

Carl soon rounded the corner and handed Smitty his Schlitz beer. Irv looked at him.

"So, what, now you think you own the place? You come over here, rob me blind, stealing all my soda, you little crook." He then smiled. Holding out his hand he said, "Put er' there partner." Irv was always trying to make the boy feel more welcomed. Carl put his small brown hand in Irv's and shook it vigorously. Then he grimaced.

"What's with kids always having sticky hands?" Smitty quietly laughed, as he was still feeling low, and his mind was far away from his friend's front porch at this moment in time. "Well, don't just stand there, go get me a beer too. Now, I gotta go wash my damn hands. I'll be right back."

The two old men talked while they drank their beers. It turned from sports to politics and then back to sports again. Irv tried talking about fishing, but Smitty quickly changed the subject to something else. Carl had wondered off and got caught up in a neighborhood soccer game, a few yards over. An hour or so later, Smitty got up from his chair.

"I'm gonna go take a piss and try to find Carl and then head out. Alright?"

"He's over at the Jenson's house, I can hear all those kids playing soccer again. They're always at it."

"Okay, thanks, I'll be right back. Thanks for the beer."

"Anytime buddy. Take it easy, will ya'?"

9

For the last remaining days of Carl's summer vacation, Smitty decided to just stay close to home, but most importantly, on dry land. They spent some of their time at the Yale Art Museum. On another day, they went over to the Peabody Museum to check out the dinosaur fossils. Carl liked to walk all the way around each and every fossil exhibit. He would slowly study each one making his mental notes, so that he could later recreate them in his drawings later. Someday, he thought to himself, "I'm gonna make a comic book with dinosaurs in it. It will be awesome!"

The art and culture of New Haven had been a great influence for Carl over the last three months. He and Smitty had visited the art museum at least eight or nine times over the summer.

Smitty couldn't exactly remember all the visits, but it seemed like a lot. Carl was teaching himself how to draw better and recreate what he observed during these visits. The paintings that he was creating were still meager, but the old man encouraged him to keep it up. He went so far as to say, that they were all "great masterpieces."

Thursday came too quickly. It was around 1:30 in the afternoon when there was a knock at the front door. Smitty got up to answer.

"Oh look, it's my favorite daughter." Carl's mom got mad and said, "Um, I'm your only daughter, Dad, or at least I hope that's the case. One never knows with you though, you and all your secrets, right?"

Smitty then had a flashback from many, many years ago when he was just in his early thirties. It was around 3a.m., and he had woke up to a young woman squatting down next to his bed, looking right at him. She looked to be about nineteen or twenty. He was startled but couldn't speak. She didn't look anything like a normal woman or human being for that matter. Her eyes were a solid black with no pupils. Her skin was a Norwegian white, like it never saw any sun before. But the most shocking thing to him was that she had birthmarks all over her skin. It had reminded him of a leopard print. "This isn't happening," he thought to himself. "It can't be real, I must be dreaming." The truth of the situation was that she was, in fact, his daughter, an extraterrestrial hybrid. They, those who are the Watchers, had taken him onboard their ship and had stolen his sperm. She was what they had created when they were playing "GOD."

All the thoughts that he was thinking were immediately answered in his head. She looked upon him like a nurse who was showing great compassion in that very moment.

In his mind, he could hear her perfectly. However, her lips never moved, it was a telepathic conversation. It was an entire conversation that had happened in a matter of seconds. This overwhelmed his simple human mind and he started to perspire. Instantly, he knew that her name was HellAnna. She was exactly six feet two inches, and her purpose was to be an architect and she was most definitely his daughter. The birth marks matched the ones he too had on his body. The feeling between them was one of love, a love that came without knowing why.

"Someday, you and I will meet again. As for this lifetime, this is the one and only time you will ever get to see me. It's for both my safety and yours. Other forces are at work here, forces you will never be able to understand. I can never come here again. My life is periodically in danger too, and I have guards who protect me now. They will keep me safe, Father."

The history of her entire life flashed through his mind, and when she finished speaking, he was shown an incubation room and the placenta sacks hanging in the room that was kept at a constant 98 degrees and lit only by a dim orange light. There was a strong smell of sulfur in the air too. This was where she had been born, or perhaps grown. The soul didn't discriminate; life is life. All it needs is a vessel.

Then she disappeared before his eyes. He laid there in bed choking back his tears and never told his wife about it. How would she understand this, he thought? How could I ever explain this to her? It doesn't make any kind of sense. For months afterwards, he was haunted by a quiet depression that no one around him ever knew about. He had written a poem about her shortly after the experience:

"Star child"

With each moment that passes
you move further away...
There are now stars between us

My father is not your father
I am only your father
from here in the now
I exist as such
But there are still stars between us

What will your day be like
when you grow up and realize
that there are stars between us?

Things are much the same for me now
as they ever were
I get up each day and live my life
with hopes, goals and aspirations
But for you, what will that even mean?
simply because, there are stars between us

My daughter, my child in the stars
I can't reach high enough
into the heavens between us

Just know one thing now
That is, that you are never forgotten
you are always in my heart
even though, there are stars between us

There was a coldness that came in the door with Carl's mom. As she crossed the threshold of her father's house, she dragged in the heavy past with her. Then she gave a quiet subdued "hello" to her father and then a quick peck on his cheek.

"You need a shave, old man." Then she quickly asked, "Where's Carl?"

"Up stairs in his bedroom packing up his things. He's got a bunch of paintings to take home too." Some were still hung up on the wall. She looked at them and noticed they made up one giant picture of an unknown star system.

"My kids got a wild imagination, doesn't he?"

"He sure does." Smitty then handed her a plain yellow envelope with her name written in all capital letters, S-A-R-A-H.

"So, what's this?"

"It's my final will. It all goes to both you and Carl, and the bond is made out to him. It's for his college education, so he can study art if he wants, or something like that. I think he's got promise, but don't tell him I said so. Don't wanna mess with the boy's ego, right?" Sarah was caught off guard and got teary-eyed. Her wall of indifference crumbled.

"Wow, you didn't have to do this! No, I can't accept." She tried to hand it back to him, but he would not take it.

"You've got no choice. I did you a great favor here with the boy. Now you gotta return it, and take this gift from me. That's the deal."

Sarah's eyes erupted in tears. The emotional trigger had been hit. She finally allowed herself to express some kind of feeling toward her father, dissolving the emotional blockade that she had put up so many years ago.

"Love you, Dad," she said, while wiping away the tears.

Pushing back her dirty blond hair, Smitty then whispered an old saying into her ear. It was one that he and Irv always used to say while drinking:

"Ashes to ashes and dust to dust, someday this old sailor will turn to rust." Only there wasn't any whiskey involved in this little reunion.

"Oh, you're an old poop, yah know that dad!" she said, while smiling back at him still wiping away the tears.

Carl had just rounded the corner and caught the tail-end of their little emotional reunion. He stopped, paused, then dropped his bags. "Hold on," he said. "I have to get the rest my artwork." His next trip back to the TV room was with a couple boxes filled with all of his cosmic art creations. "Wow," his mother said. "You've been really busy making art this summer, huh?"

Carl quietly responded "Yes, I guess so." In that moment, he seemed very despondent and sad to be leaving Smitty. The human bond that he was leaving behind, the one that he had formed with the old man, meant more than anything else in the whole world to him. In a way it felt like his father leaving all over again. He was looking at his mother, remembering the secrets he had been entrusted with. Smitty had smiled looking down at him and raised his pointer finger to his pursed lips, making a shushing sound. He mouthed to Carl, "the secret." He nodded a simple 'yes' in response, moving his head up and down. Sarah failed to catch the signal as she looked through Carl's artwork. Smitty said his goodbyes in his old manly way and gave them each a standoffish awkward hug before they left.

And now Carl was on his way back to the city and on his way to discovering a new version of himself. He now had a new sense of self-worth, thanks to the old man. The world looked a little less scary and he was now a little braver. Little did his mother know, he also had a few more curse words in his vernacular too.

10

It was the summer of 1998 in Long Island City, New York. A tall and lanky light-brown skinned man stood alone in his art studio, hunched over a drawing board in deep thought. A set of colorful frames were laid out before him. As usual, they were arranged in a strict order. This man, who was now twenty-five years old, was no longer a boy. He was now both the writer and the artist. Despite some opposition, he had forged ahead and created the road before him. It was the path that he had desired to create, one of self-fortitude and determination. A wise old man had once told him, "These are the times that define a man's soul, and if you do not ascend to your greatest potential in life, all you shall know is a lifetime of pain."

The old GE air-conditioner was singing on high. An oscillating fan was also part of the battle, pushing cool air back and forth across the room. The stifling heat was well over ninety degrees outside. The pavement on the street below was even hotter. Just like the old cliché says:

"So hot you could fry an egg on it." All the AC units appeared out the side of the old brownstones like an obtuse buzzing mechanical protrusion. Each pedestrian that walked below was dotted with the random drops of condensation falling from them, giving to the feeling of being spit upon.

Carl told himself that it was yet another day that was hotter than Hell. He then had flashbacks to the summer of '84. He remembered the old man and all of his kindness, too. But in the same thought, he remembered "THEM," and then the mood turned sour. It was just two weeks before that he had made the requested phone call that Smitty had asked him to do, all those years ago. As promised, he made it, and kept the secret alive in his heart. He was staring at his drawing in a mindless daze when there was a loud knock at his studio door. Jerking forward, it had scared the shit out of him. Looking through the peep hole, he could see it was two well-dressed men in black suits. He opened the door until the security chain stopped it from swinging out all the way. "Yes?" he inquired.

"Are you Carl Smith?" one of them asked.

"Yes, that's me, why?"

"Did you order potato chips?"

"Um, yes, I did." He then pushed the door forward, so he could remove the security chain.

"Please, come in."

The two men entered the studio with an old-fashioned steamer trunk. It was placed in the very center of the room so that they were all separated by thirds. They looked at him, nodded, and then silently walked out the door like they were never there. Carl rushed to the door, sliding back the security chain and then locked the dead bolt for good measure. "No one can know," he thought to himself. The sweat from his hidden anxiety was beading up on his forehead now. His mind was swimming in the thoughts of what the old man had once shown him. He had been waiting all this time to do just this one thing. Dropping to his knees, he removed a small red pouch from his front pocket. In it was an old brass key, the kind you see in small boxes at yard sales. With a slow and steady precision, he turned the key and opened the old chest.

A new story, in all of its various components laid there before him. The one last true story that had to be told. He could almost hear Smitty's voice in his ear saying, "The world must know about 'THEM'."

PART II

• • ○ • •

**There are those who see their destiny
written in the stars, and for all the others;
it is simply in the way of things.**

1

There was a city that was filled with millions of busy people. Each who felt alone and isolated while living in such close proximity with one another. Desperate souls. Lost souls. A tidal pool filled with creative potential.

Silently, in the corner of an upper east-side brown stone apartment, was an old oak desk. This desk had seen the rigors of time. There had been grandparents, mothers, fathers and children who had all learned both the alphabet and math on it; a legacy of knowledge. All the letters of the alphabet were carved into it. This was a reminder of the many lifetimes that had preserved its affluence; an object frozen in time, a perfect stillness with an antiquity.

Upon the weathered writing table was an off-white legal pad. There was also a mug that said "World's best Dad" on it. It was an old stained coffee mug that held pens, pencils and an old pair of sewing scissors. These were the implements of creative virtue. What nobody knew was there was a key sitting at the very bottom of the mug. It was hidden both in and out of plain sight.

By the time Tara had gotten back to the apartment, her father, Barry, had already left for his afternoon walk. She imagined him still being there, and visualized him running the same boring routine: getting his pack of smokes that sat in his upper left hand pocket, putting on a 1970's tarnished TIMEX watch, wearing a pair of pressed khaki trousers and his faded denim jacket that had a P.O.W. patch on its sleeve.

Before he had left, however, out of politeness, he wrote a note for Tara, simply because she always worried if he would ever come back. Barry also suffered from the occasional cognitive issues from the war. Tara suspected it was from the Agent Orange, which was used to defoliate the jungle canopy in Vietnam.

They now relied heavily on one another, and they were each integral in each other's lives. This father daughter pair were kind of like an old pair of sneakers hanging from the telephone wires out in the street, exposed to all the elements of life. They weathered what ever the world threw at them together.

The note briefly read: *"Dearest Daughter, I'm off on another adventure, be back by dinner. Love, Dad."*

With a rustle of loose pocket change, Barry stepped out onto the front steps of his brownstone and then locked the apartment door. It was a faded forest green, and he cursed at it, as if it were a foreign adversary whenever he left. He would say: "Jesus Christ! Get a new coat of paint will yah!" And the door fought back and stuck in its swollen jamb from the humidity. This caused Barry to pull with all his weight. Each match they fought was accompanied by a fit of arthritic pain afterwords. He then descended down the crumbling brownstone steps onto the streets of Harlem saying to himself again, "Stupid fucking door." Simple life frustrations got him upset.

2

It was late September, 1999. President Clinton was all over the news after his affair with Monica Lewinski, and the Russians were fighting off Islamic extremists in their outer territories. But all anyone could talk about was the "Black Dress." And there were three large glowing orange lights that silently floated over D.U.M.B.O. one night. This news never got reported. The residents of New York City talked about it, and wondered, why? When some residents approached the local broadcasters, all they heard in return was silence.

The normal city chaos was in perfect working order. Another day, another week, in another year. Barry was standing at the Bodega reading the NY Daily News, when the man behind the counter irked him by saying: "Hey, you gonna buy it or what. News ain't free, buddy." To which Barry responded back, "I've wasted better men than you in Nam, shithead." The clerk quickly looked away and pretended that he had more important business to attended to. Barry then placed the coffee cup down on the stand, being careful as he fought his hand tremors. Using his left hand, his pocket finally released the loose change from its grasp. Then he was finally able to get his fifty five cents out. With a sense of attitude, Barry slapped the change down onto the counter top. Then he stuck out his hand like he was holding a pistol and said: "Bang, now it's yours sucka'."

When the weather permitted, Barry would often head downtown to Union Square Park by way of the six train and play chess with the other "Brothers," as he liked to call them. After his two tours in Nam, he liked to stick with his own kind. Whitey wasn't so friendly to him in his Army days, even though they were fighting on the same side. He could often be quoted saying, "It's bad blood from now on. I stick to my own kind."

After getting his coffee and paper, Barry headed back home to sit out in front of his apartment, read the paper and sip his coffee for a while. He was on permanent disability now and was cleared by the VA from a head trauma. Life was now one long vacation with a little extra money from Uncle Sam every month.

Rounding the corner, taking his sweet precious time, Barry stood at the corner of 3rd Avenue and 106th Street waiting for the crosswalk light to turn. Many yellow cabs drove on past, one after another, a sea of yellow. The city buses and mail trucks filled the air with their dark gray exhaust fumes. And here, all the city people from the many walks of life, clogged the sidewalks.

Barry turned to drop his cup in the trash can when he began to experience a sharp ringing in both ears. He was haunted by his war injury and was now taking meds prescribed by the VA. He clutched both ears and clenched his fists as a searing pain pierced his skull. The pain sometimes caused nausea and momentary blurred vision when he had an episode such as this. Today, it was something else...

Looking out across the avenue, a long purple shadow moved over the street. The normal street noise faded away into a static crackle, then a 1935 yellow Ford Coup drove by and blew its horn making an odd buzzzaa sound, followed by an angry mob of negro protesters making its way down the avenue. All the while, a boy stood on the corner selling newspapers to each of the passerby. He too, held up a single paper, yelling "hot news!"

"What the hell is this," Barry thought to himself? "Somebody must be filming a movie or something? Where the fuck am I?"

He quickly looked back to his side of the street, and it was the normal 1990's buses and taxis. He looked back to the other side, and it was a 1930's scene being played out. The ringing hit him once more, which forced him to double over and vomit onto the sidewalk. He splattered chewed up egg and cheese with a splash of coffee all over his Red-Wing work boots.

After he looked up again, the movie scene had vanished, like it was never there. He thought to himself, "How do I explain this one? I've seen some really weird shit, but this takes the cake. I'm going write this down in my notes when I get back to the apartment."

Later that evening, Tara came home to find her dad crashing on the sofa listening to some of his old Herbie Hancock records -the older stuff from the 60's. The song *Cantaloupe Island* was playing just as she walked through the door. Tara made an angry face as the smell hit her nose.

"Jesus, Dad, smells like a bar in here. How many beers have you had? And what is that other smell, vomit?" Barry opened his eyes. They were blood shot and blurry now.

"I had an episode today, barfed my breakfast all over the sidewalk. I don't know what hit me, but I think I hallucinated or something. Or, maybe, I'm just losing my mind."

"Why, what happened? Do I need to call the VA again? Are your meds not working?"

"No, no, this one started off like all the other episodes, except after the ringing in my ears, everything went dead silent. Even worse, I was looking across the avenue, and I couldn't believe what I was seeing! On one side of the street there was 1999, and on the other side was the 1930s. I stood there and watched the 1935 race riot! Then this searing pain went through my head, and I threw up my breakfast. It was over after that. Soon as I came to, the world went back to normal. I'm living in an episode of the X-Files!" Tara's motherly instincts immediately kicked in.

"Well, go wash up, and I'll straighten up in here and make some dinner for us. And wash those damn boots!" She had chosen not to dive any deeper into the matter. Sometimes when she did, Barry got really agitated and screamed at her. Today she knew he could be easily triggered.

3

It was 3:30a.m. and Carl was dead asleep in his Brooklyn loft apartment. He laid there with just a thin white cotton sheet covering his long lanky body. The white noise machine was on to block out the usual neighborhood street noises happening below. A small figure stood in the shadows of his bedroom, and it was consciously observing his inner dreaming. In his mind, he could see an incubator room aboard a mother-ship with all the hybrid babies in it. The room was dark, except for the soft glow of soft orange lights. It smelled of rotten eggs. Psychically, he had connected with one of the odd looking babies, which was suspended in a large glass looking vessel. It had a large head on a human looking body. Then a voice in his mind said, "This one is yours, Carl. These are your hybrids. They are to be our future assets. They will be spread out among the stars, those that survive." Then there was a very tall and lanky alien-like creature that had twig-like arms and legs who walked in to check on the babies, and the dream abruptly ended there.

Carl woke up, bit his lip and screamed. A cold sweat was dripping from his forehead. The white cotton sheets stuck to his sweaty body. Just then he saw the small figure quickly faded away into nothing but darkness. He wondered afterwards if the experience was real or not. Was it a dream? Was I really there? Or maybe both were in fact true.

Getting out of bed, he turned on the light and made sure his closet door was still closed. Sometimes they liked to come out of there, he thought to himself. His night clothes were still on his body correctly. They didn't make that mistake again. After such events, Carl made it a habit to turn on absolutely every single light in his apartment, making it feel like daytime. This would make him feel safe again.

Carl naturally assumed he wouldn't be sleeping anymore, so he made himself strong black coffee and toast. Alone, he sat there making notes in his journal. He thought of the old man just then. Flash backs of his childhood came flooding in. There were the fishing trips, Cote's Diner, new clothes, trips to Gillete Castle and the beautiful Connecticut River Valley. There was also a love and nostalgia for these thoughts which quickly turned into a remorse as he also thought about "THEM." Even while sitting there in reflection, Carl was still trying to recall events from this night. Sitting there, he could remember a bright red light that appeared just behind his bedroom door. It had woken him up, but then he kept having a dream within a dream, and couldn't wake up. He realized that something had trapped his thoughts in an endless loop, like being held underwater.

The only escape from these crazy alien dreams was his art. Carl had started doing freelance work for some AD companies in the city. It was good money and helped pay the rent. He was also now engaged in drawing his own comic books series titled: "PARA-DOX." It covered a lot of the material that the "old man" had passed on to him. Through this medium, he could safely leak out all the horrible secrets that the government was sitting on. There were Nazis in the U.S., UFO's over Chicago, numerous night time abductions, ghost soldiers, cattle mutilations and time-slips. He had so many paranormal ideas to work with. The expression was limitless.

These comic books also came to be an outlet for his own E.T. contact experiences. There were a few small beings that he called the "Mechanics." It was they that came and retrieved him from his apartment about every six months or so. During these events, he was receiving information about the universe and how all things were connected, the tapestry of the universe, all things being one. He was also part of the breeding programs where they collected his semen to make hybrids. This part of the contact experience didn't sit well with him. It sometimes felt akin to rape. But, they always seemed nice and gentle during such procedures, which unnerved Carl. Their limited range of emotions were so different from his own. They didn't seem locked into our ability to emotionally feel everything. There was an inhuman coldness. They said they understood, but somehow that didn't feel true. They were devoid of emotions.

Later that morning at around 9a.m., there was a knock at the door. Carl got up from his drawing table and looked out of the peephole to see a delivery boy standing there. He opened the door and signed for the expected package. The box contained the latest issue, (Number 14) of PARA-DOX. This issue was titled, "Time-Slip." On the cover was a T-Rex dinosaur with a Nazi UFO in its mouth. With every issue that came out, Carl was beaming with pride, even if he didn't sell a lot of them. He was simply happy that there were a few fan boy collectors who avidly followed his work.

When Carl was feeling uncreative or had writer's block, he would often go to one of the many parks in Manhattan and work amongst the people. Simply overhearing a conversation would spark an idea to create something both weird and original. The city had many interesting characters that were unique only to New York.

Today, after his "Hybrid" experience, was one such day. He headed over to Union Square on the L-train with his drawing pad and pencils. Hopefully, while there, he could refresh his imagination and create something out of last night's disturbing experience. And there he sat, across from the brothers playing chess, when all of a sudden one of them got up and yelled, "Fuck you, Jack!" The man then flipped the chess board, tossing pieces everywhere and stormed off across the court. The other man cleaned up the mess. Carl could see that he was laughing at what just went down. The man then came over to where Carl was sitting, made himself comfortable and lit his cigarette. He turned to Carl.

"Did you see that shit? That brother was crazy! I launched a Dutch Defense on his ass, never saw it coming." Then he laughed with an arrogant pride. It seemed as if he were talking to himself, when he said: "Even a pawn can win the war." He turned back to Carl and kept talking.

"Say, what are you drawing there, young brotha?" Carl leaned over and showed him the drawing from last night's event with the huge alien test-tube babies. The man's eyes got really big, like he recognized something in them. Carl could see fear in his eyes.

"You into that science fiction stuff, huh?" Carl politely responded.

"Yes, I write and draw my own comic books series. You want to see one?"

"Yeah, sure of course." Carl reached into his messenger bag and handed him the new issue, #14 "Time-Slip." The stranger was silent for a while as he leafed through the book. Then he looked back to Carl once more with a menthol cigarette hanging off the end of his lips.

"You draw pretty good, kid. I've seen some weird shit like this too, when I was over in Nam. I was out on patrol, and we found a cave that we suspected the Vietcong was in. So I volunteered to go in after them. All I had was my .38 Special, a knife and a flash light. Then another guy followed me in, staying about twelve feet behind. This was just in case there was any booby-traps. The VC had all sorts of inventions to give us hell. Worst of all, I was in a confined space, with nowhere to run. You had to take it head on, no matter what came at you. Those Gooks were some tricky mother fuckers!"

"So when were you in Nam?"

"1968. It was during the Tet Offensive. Charlie came at us from everywhere, like nothing you'd ever seen. It was Hell on earth. Small and large groups attacked Saigon and our air bases too. It was days of fighting in close quarters, building to building in some cases. I served two tours over there. The second tour I was going out with the tunnel rats, as back up support. I'm too big to fit down any of those Gook holes, man." The man then bit down on his cigarette as if he were reliving the pain. Carl took note of his anxiety.

After hearing the details of the man's story, Carl reached over to shake hands with the stranger.

"I'm Carl, by the way." The man happily reached back.

"I'm Barry, nice to meet ya' kid. Thanks for the comic book. I'll read it tonight, promise."

"It was nice meeting you Barry. I gotta get going. I'll see you around. Take care." Barry waved as Carl walked off across the park not looking back.

4

It was around 7p.m. when Tara got home from work Wednesday night. She had gone in around six in the morning and was asked to stay later than usual to help a few trauma victims. There were a few people who were involved in a head on collision. The ER was packed, and there was no walking away. Mandatory over-time.

Coming in the door, she looked totally exhausted. Barry was on the couch reading the comic book and looked up at his exhausted daughter.

"Look what the cat dragged in. You look tired, girl. I wrapped a plate of food and put it in the fridge for you, Tara."

"Oh, you're too nice, thanks. It was murder at work today, literally." She quickly noticed the comic book.

"Aren't you a little old for that kind of stuff, Dad?"

"Who me? No, never too old." Feeling anxious, Barry blurted out, "I had an altercation at the chess board, after I launched a sneak attack on Carlos today. He blew up, cursed me out, flipped the board and walked away. It was great! Oh, and then I talked to one of those big headed brothers. He makes comic books, and they're really weird shit."

"I bet you told him all about being in the war, too?"

"Yes, of course I did. It's my life. It's interesting. And besides, he seemed really keen on hearing war stories for some reason."

"Well, as long as you didn't bore him with all your Civil War history facts. That's all in the past Dad. Nobody cares anymore. And don't you dare say it!"

"Say what? "Those who forget history are doomed to repeat it?"

"Yes, that! Gosh... Let the past, stay in the past. History doesn't pay the rent here."

Both Barry and Tara sat across from each other at the small kitchen table, which was barely big enough for the two of them. Barry drank his Heineken, and Tara ate her fried chicken, rice and some fried okra. Tara broke the silence.

"Tell you what, Dad. You shoulda' been a chef or something. You've got skills in the kitchen, old man."

"Thanks baby girl, I try." Having been put on permanent disability for his migraines, Barry was feeling very insecure about pulling his own weight. Regular weekly paychecks weren't coming in now. Barry only did the occasional jobs for the building Super, cash in hand. Tara was now the bread winner. Aside from that, Barry only had his disability checks from Uncle Sam. And to add insult to injury, he had to lawyer up against the VA to get the disability checks going. He blamed all the white doctors their, it was more than obvious to him.

Later that evening, Barry was sitting on the couch looking at Carl's comic book again. What struck him was that it was describing something similar to what he had seen in his 1930's vision. He thought to himself, "So I wasn't just making this shit up? This thing that happened, actually had a name, a time-slip? I guess that's what people must be seeing on the old Civil War battlefields when they report seeing ghost troops there. So strange, so very strange. I've gotta talk to Carl again. He'll want to hear my story."

Barry went upstairs to his writing desk and wrote a letter that was addressed to Carl's post office box, which was listed on the back of his comic book.

"Dear Carl,

This is Barry, the "chess player." I met you the other day in Union Square Park after that Brotha' flipped out and tossed the chess board. You and I briefly spoke about Nam, too. Your new comic book story about a "Time-Slip" was very interesting. I had something like this happen to me recently, but I didn't know what it was called, or that it even happened to other people. Write me back at this return address. We should meet and talk."

Best Regards,

Barry Jones

5

Carl sat at his drawing board thinking about his "hybrid baby" dream again. Sitting next to him were the sketches of the test-tube babies. Having a dream within a dream was now haunting him. He wondered how he could weave this into a comic book story. The story of the "Mind Prisoner" or "The children of lost" sounded good to him.

Thinking aloud to himself, "I've got it! I'll tell a story about a man who is stuck in an endless dream. He'll keep waking up in a different era and have to figure out that he is still dreaming. In the dreams, he'll always feel like he's being watched too. The presence will be a woman, but he can't see her. She'll be the only thing that gives him any comfort. At the end of each dream he'll see the numbers 45-454. There's a hidden message in the numbers, that's driving him mad, because he can't figure it out."

Around 2:00, Carl walked away from the drawing board, deciding that he had had enough. The creative voice in his head had gone silent. "Know when to say when," he thought to himself. Anyway, it's time to get the mail and eat some lunch before I forget to eat again.

Making his way from the elevator to the postal box, Carl noticed for the first time today that the weather outside was now conducive for taking a walk. It was time to hunt for some inspiration out in the real world.

Sometimes Carl felt very out of touch with everyone else because of the experiences he'd had as a boy. Those people out there had the luxury of leading "normal or simple" lives. They didn't carry the burden of experiencing the multiverse like he did. He felt envious of them. There was something beautiful in being ignorant to the super-natural.

The seventies style hallway light overhead burned out in that moment, and the daydream ended there.

Carl stood before the brass plated postal box #333 and then gave the key a slow grinding turn to open it up. Sometimes it took some coercion to open because it was so old. It had never been replaced because the landlord was too cheap, but so was the rent. There was only one piece of mail today. A letter from Mr. Barry Jones. Carl immediately became curious knowing that it was most likely from Barry, the chess player.

First thing he noticed was that the return address was from Harlem, New York. Sitting at his kitchen table, he read the letter while eating his ham and cheese sandwich with extra mustard. After reading the letter, Carl enthusiastically wrote Barry back that same afternoon.

"Dear Barry,

It was nice meeting you the other day as well. I always love to hear stories like yours. Very often, I will include such ideas as a story line in my comic book "PARA-DOX." I make it a point to include as many real and relevant paranormal stories as I can. If you're going to share your stories… the weirder, the better, please. So let's get together and talk in person again. My phone number is 212-789-X021."

Best Regards,

Carl Smith

It was Wednesday morning when Barry decided to finally call Carl. Two weeks had passed since he had mailed the letter, so he wasn't sure if he would ever call him back. The phone rings.

"Hello, is this Para-dox Studios." a raspy voice asked, sounding off key.

"Yes, it is."

"Hey kid, this is Barry from the park. How are ya'?"

"All things considered, I'm alive and well, I guess."

"You free around two o'clock tomorrow? We can meet, and I'll finish the story about the cave incident. There was something I didn't tell you. Something that will mess with your mind, man." Carl hesitated for a few moments, until Barry spoke again.

"Hello, you still there?"

"Yes, yes, I'm still here. I was just thinking, sorry. Yes, I got your return address on the envelope, I'll stop by your place tomorrow. You drink beer?"

"Yes, of course. See you then." Barry abruptly hung up the phone. Carl had been around enough of the phenomenon to know when something felt off kilter. Barry's tone seemed very nervous, like he was hesitating, or maybe he was hiding something. He couldn't be sure, but it kind of felt like "THEM." They had that effect on people. It left people feeling very ungrounded, too.

6

The next day, Carl made his way over to the L-Train. There was the usual tribe of tattooed twenty somethings from Brooklyn waiting for the train together. They all had the same "anti-style." The platform was covered in random graffiti, and it smelled of piss. Carl took the train into Manhattan and then transferred to the 5-train going uptown into Harlem. While Carl was riding the subway, it made the usual express stops along the way. He would often read comic books when riding the train to kill time. For him, it was always awkward sitting across from the other riders who were just staring at each other. There was nothing to do but stare and pretend not to make eye contact.

The faceless people repeatedly got on and off the train and went about their daily business, millions of people who didn't care to know each other. The one thing that stood out on the train was a homeless man who was passed out face first on the floor. He laid there directly under the subway car bench. A long forgotten man. When Carl got off at his stop, he found a cop and told him what he had seen.

"He might be dead! Yes, on the north bound 5-train, that was the one. He had on a green khaki jacket too."

The cop looked at him and just laughed. People in the city were so jaded he thought, especially the ones who never left it. They all became numb to its eviscerating clutches. In some Brooklyn neighborhoods, there were people who never left their own block. It was a prison within a prison, a subset of a culture that existed nowhere else but here.

Carl arrived in Harlem at around 2:30 as planned. He made an extra stop at the local Bodega to pick up a six-pack of Bud for him and Barry to drink.

Standing before the ominous green door, Carl suddenly got the chills again. He thought to himself once more. "Is it? Yes, it's definitely "THEM." He then fought back his own fears about what may or may not be here in this space. Then in his minds eye he saw two big black eyes, and it was confirmed.

After the third knock, the door finally opened up to a small two floor apartment. Barry greeted Carl and invited him in. Stepping over the threshold, Carl knew that he would have to be on-point, and read between the lines. There was information that he most certainly wanted. Looking around, he noticed that this small two floor apartment was well kept, like it had a lady's touch. Everything was typical: A modest TV set, a Realistic brand record player, a floral patterned couch and a writing desk off in the corner. Toward the back there was a tiny kitchen.

Carl and Barry shook hands, like they were ready to go to war together. However, Carl noticed that Barry looked tired and rough. Seeing his face he thought that maybe he hadn't shaved for a few days. Barry wasted no time and got right down to it.

"Grab a seat kid. I'll go get the bottle opener." He quickly returned, grabbed a beer, popped the top and drained most of it in one gulp. Carl thought to himself, "This guy is really on the edge! We better make sure we take the conversation slowly so I don't provoke him too much. Maybe he's got post war shock or something."

Both men sat there looking at one another for a few moments before Carl broke the silence.

"So, you mind if I use my tape recorder? I don't want to miss any of the details from your cave story." Barry didn't seem to care.

"Yeah, that's not a problem. Do what ya' gotta do." Carl then cautiously proceeded.

"So, you mentioned the other day in the park after you saw my comic book that you "saw some weird shit" in Nam. Can you tell me about that?" Barry then leaned over the coffee table and grabbed a cigarette from his pack of KOOLS. Carl could tell he was taking his time to gather his own thoughts before speaking. Finally, Barry released a puff of smoke and said,

"Well, we found this jungle cave while patrolling the border of Cambodia. The captain then looked at me and said, "Tag, you're it, Jones." So I was the front man, like I said the other day. John Baker backed me up and came in twelve or so feet behind, keeping a safe distance. We walked back into that cave at a snail's pace for a good fifteen or twenty minutes, and then it happened. I flashed the light up ahead of me, after I thought I heard something rustle. It sounded like a muted squeak or something. When I brought the light beam back to my far left, there were these four huge blue eyes looking back at me. Startled, I started firing my .38 but hit nothing. These two beings looked right through me. John then caught up to me and saw them too. I heard their voices in my mind. They said, "We are Gibbens." They had three fingers on their hands and three toes on their feet. Their skin was a fleshy white, like an albino dolphin. Both of us were completely frozen as they spoke. John could hear them in his head too. Then they said,

"We mean you no harm. Leave this cave now." Then they turned and walked right through the fucking stone cave wall. Soon as they disappeared, I threw up! I then looked back to John. Shining my light in his face I said,

"We didn't see this. This never fucking happened. Got it?" John nodded back at me. When we came out of the cave about an hour later, the guys were asking if we killed any Gooks. I said it was just rats and I had to shoot at them. Carl was very curious now and leaning in over the coffee table.

"What do you think they were? Were they aliens or something?" "No, I don't think so but then again, I've never seen any little green men from Mars. So how would I know? After they were in my mind, I felt so violated. It was as if my sense of reality had been destroyed forever. I couldn't look at the other guys when I got out of the cave. All I could think of was that none of this made sense. The war made no sense either. I had no desire left in me to fight. It wasn't too much longer after that that a mortar round gave me a severe brain injury, and I was sent home. Got a Purple Heart medal and all that business. Then I had to deal with the stupid hippies protesting when I got back home to the states! Let... me... tell... you... Unless you've been in the war, you've got nothing to say about it as far as I'm concerned. Men have been killing men, since the beginning of time."

Carl looked at Barry while taking a sip of his beer and then nodded in agreement with his latter statement. Barry's face looked a little pale, so Carl suggested that they take a walk outside to cool off for a bit. Getting up off the couch, Barry handed Carl the keys and asked him to lock the door behind them. Carl noticed his hands were shaking.

Carl walked slowly alongside Barry as they headed up 3rd Avenue. It was filled with the usual food joints, hairdressers and electronics shops that sold one of everything. No matter where you went in the city, they all seemed to look the same. The streets were filled with people, and the roads were clogged with traffic. All the same stuff. The passerby didn't look at them. Everyone was a stranger. Suddenly Barry stopped and pointed to the corner of 106th.

"Yes, that's the place, Carl. That is where I saw it happen."

"Where what happened?"

"It's where I saw the "time-slip." Just like in your comic book. On this side of the road it was 1999, and over on that side it was 1935. I saw an old Ford Coupe and then there were these protesters marching. It was the 1935 race riot happening! I couldn't believe my own eyes. Then I had this harsh ringing in my ears, and when I looked back, it was all gone. Thought I was losing my God damn mind!"

Carl quickly asked, "So, how long did this vision of yours last?"

"It was only a matter of minutes, and it felt so real! You think I'm nuts, don't ya'?"

"Trust me, I don't. Hey, let me walk you back home, Barry." Carl could sense that Barry was becoming very agitated. He was clenching his fists and sweating. On the way back, Carl had him sit on a park bench and rest for a minutes. He thought to himself that if this guy didn't take a breather, he was going to have a massive stroke or something.

Both Carl and Barry made their way back to his brownstone apartment and sat down to talk a little more. Carl pointedly looked at Barry.

"You know something, Barry, I've had my own weird experiences too. You're not alone. That's why I started writing my comic book, "PARA-DOX." I needed to have some sort of outlet for the crazy shit I was seeing. And trust me when I say, you just can't talk about this stuff with the average person either. People would have me committed if they knew about the things that I've seen and heard." Barry abruptly got up and went to the kitchen for another round of beers. Carl looked down at his tape recorder and noticed that it had reached the end of the tape. He took it out and flipped it over, so he could continue the recording session.

Barry was once again sitting across from Carl, and he got quiet all of a sudden. Carl could tell he was thinking about something deep or maybe even painful just by the expression on his face. Perhaps it was another secret, or he was still stressed talking about his alien encounter. Then he thought, maybe these beings were some sort of Crypted, an unidentified species that no one had discovered yet, like a Big-Foot.

Still agitated, Barry got up again, walked over to his writing desk and dumped out the jar of pens and pencils onto the table. A small sheet-metal key came out after everything else. He picked up the key and held it up for Carl to see.

"This is it. The key of secrets." Carl looked at him and shrugged his shoulders. He wasn't sure where this conversation was headed. Barry then got down on his hands and knees and stuck his arm under the couch. It was obvious that he was digging around for something. After a minute or two, he located what he was after. He came back up with a brown metal cashier's box. He looked up at Carl and then proceeded to open it. Carl leaned over and looked with great curiosity. He then had a flashback to when Smitty opened his secret wall compartment and pulled out the potato chip tin filled with top-secret files, treasures of curiosity. A hidden story.

In this box, there were some old photos, war time postcards and a few handwritten notes. There was also a tarnished revolver with S&W hallmarked on its side. Barry then looked up to Carl.

"Look at these pictures! Check this shit out." He handed Carl a few black and white photos. He could see that they were taken from a gun ship during the Vietnam War. Off in the distance there were two UFOs shaped like triangles. Carl looked back to Barry and waited for him to explain. Barry took his time, lit another cigarette and paused for a moment longer. Carl could see that Barry was reliving the moment. He had that far lost look in his eyes.

"I was riding along with my buddy Ned. He was on the fifty caliber gun with the Razor Backs. They provided air support to the ground troops in case we got pinned down by the VC. They would go out two or three times a day and took fire nearly every time. Those guys had balls! I was the one who took these photos." He then went on to say,

"So, there were these UFOs. Three of them. The pilot pointed them out to me; he knew I had my camera going. Afterwards, he said he'd seen the "Foo-Fighters" a few times during the war. He felt that he was being watched by them somehow. Anytime he spotted them, he'd have bad nightmares after that. I've never forgotten it though. Some things like that can bother a man forever, of this I am sure." Carl was trying to hide his excitement. This would be amazing material for him to work from.

"Barry, do you think there was a connection between the Gibbens you saw in the cave and the UFOs?" Barry sat there and had this thousand yard stare. It was plain to see that he was lost in his memories, maybe searching for something. Carl took his time, sipped his beer and let Barry mull over the question for a bit. A few minutes later, Barry finally spoke.

"You know something, Carl, that's a good question. I would never have thought to even have connected the two. You might be on to something, kid." Just as Barry finished talking, there was a rustle at the front door. Barry made no effort to react. Tara had come home from work and looked exhausted as usual. She immediately locked eyes with Carl. There was an immediate connection that was unspoken for. She smiled flirtatiously and used her free hand to fix her hair. A moment of self consciousnesses.

"Dad, don't be rude. Please introduce me to your friend."

"Carl, this is my daughter, Tara." Carl extended his hand. Tara noted how slender and muscular his arms were then. His physical form stirred her emotions. They locked eyes then.

"Very nice to meet you, Tara." She jokingly quipped.

"Are you that big-headed brotha' that writes the comic books that my dad has been babbling on about?" Carl felt embarrassed by her jab.

"Yep, that would be me."

"So, are you really into all this weird psychic paranormal stuff too?"

"Yes, that's my life, for better or worse. The world is a strange place with lots of unexplainable things in it. Not to sound too cliche, but we're not alone." Then Tara turned her back to him while reaching for her dad's cigarettes. She locked eyes again with Carl while she lit it, as if to say, I'm still interested.

"Uh huh, sure, right. My dad's shared his stories with me too. I only half believe that kinda' stuff. They did a lot drugs over there in Nam. Did he tell you that part? The pot, opium, hash, and acid, etc. They were out in the jungle tripping balls on LSD chasing after Charlie. God only knows how they didn't end up killing each other. Somebody will make a movie out of that one day." Carl looked over to Barry. His imagination stirring.

"No, your dad didn't tell me that part, at least not yet." And then he noticed Barry was rolling his eyes at his daughter and shaking his head. Carl could see that he was mad that she mentioned this fact. Tara let out a good and almost mean laugh then. Barry looked at her and mouthed, "you bitch!" She laughed at his imply, holding her hand to her mouth.

"Enough of this voo-doo talk. What's for dinner, Dad, or are we just drinking beer for dinner tonight?" Barry then had to confess to his daughter that he had lost track of time and hadn't done a single thing for dinner.

Tara seemed a little aggravated now, "So tonight it will be "Chinese takeout."

Carl was invited to stay for some take-out food and happily agreed. The three of them sat around for quite some time getting to know each other. Tara was just happy that her father was socializing and maybe venting out some of the trauma that haunted him from the war. As for Carl, he was refilling his well of creativity with Barry's war stories. He hadn't been this excited for quite some time. It was almost 9:00 at night before Carl excused himself to go home. He had a long night of writing ahead of him. All his best work was done in the early hours of the morning.

7

It was after 10:00 when Carl finally arrived back home. He dropped his messenger bag over by the drafting table, and quickly made a pot of strong coffee. Lots of caffeine was needed, the fuel that drives inspiration. Like always, he proceeded to eat a snickers bar in three bites before setting off to his work.

Around 1a.m. Carl sat down to write up some more notes after having listened to his tape-recording of Barry's paranormal war story. Carl's notes read.

-There is fact, there is proof and there is a fictitious play here. The paranormal hinges on the periphery of lunacy and imagination. Somewhere in between lies the truth.
-In that gray area that lies in between, we are to find the actual transcendental truth of our reality. It goes well beyond the confines of this 3D matrix that we are encapsulated in.

-Only 31% of people in the United States know their neighbors, so how are we ever to know our star relatives? As a species, we are self-centered and self-absorbed to the point that the world barely exists around us. But then, there is the quantum field. In that, everything exists. So we can't say that these things aren't real. They may just not exist in our current matrix. The bigger question is, what is holding all of this together? What is the greater thought of creation?
-I think I'm being blocked from a lot of my own abduction memories, and Barry probably is too. I suspect that they've somehow put up a partition in my mind. It blocks off my conscious self from knowing it all. We are not ready to know it all, no, not yet. These human minds are much to feeble.

While Carl worked, it was around the same time that Barry woke up from another one of his nightmares. He was drenched in sweat. The last thing he remembered was the Gibbens standing in his room looking over him. He felt like they were there to study him. None of his thoughts were private. They were digging around in his mind for information about Carl. There was no safety and there was no fighting it. It was A war that couldn't be fought with guns.

Barry went downstairs guided only by a dim nightlight. He was after a drink of milk. As he opened up the refrigerator, its light caught the eyes of one of the visitors before it quickly disappeared. Both fear and anxiety were moving in on Barry. Trying to calm his nerves, he opted to take a shot of Wild Turkey instead. Sitting there alone in the dark at the kitchen table, he could feel them in his mind. They were trying to tell him that it was all okay. But was it? Barry wasn't having any of it. This ends tonight he told them. I will fight back!

Turning on the light, Barry sat down at the old writing table. He grabbed a pen and legal pad, and started writing:

"The spirit of man is mean and wicked. The only Devil here is the one looking back at me in the mirror. And the only real war is the one that I wage upon myself. When a man kills another man, he is only killing himself. I think all things should end where they began, and I am finished with this world now. I am finished with this war tonight. Good bye."

Barry got up from his writing table and went to retrieve his .38 Special. He then took another shot of whiskey before going into the bathroom. Sitting in the bathtub wearing only a t-shirt and boxer shorts, the porcelain tub felt cold against his skin, but that somehow seemed irrelevant. Cold sweat dripped down his forehead stinging his eyes. All he could see was himself in the cave with those large blue eyes looking back at him. They were penetrating his mind. Desperate to make the painful memory stop, Barry put the cold steel barrel into his mouth and pulled the trigger. When he did, all he heard was a click. He pulled it again, and all he heard was another click. Then again, click-click-click. The fear and horror were not to be ended tonight. He got up out of the tub, got himself dressed and walked until first sunlight. Along the way, he dropped the revolver down into the storm drain where no one would find it for decades.

A few weeks later, Carl called Barry on the phone to discuss their last interview, but no one answered. Carl's gut feeling told him something was wrong. Instinctively he showed up at Barry's apartment later that evening out of concern. Ringing the bell a few times, Tara finally answered the door and the invited Carl inside. He noticed she had a long face and seemed very sad about something. He couldn't be sure about what. When they both sat down, Tara looked at him and said,

"Hey, I got some bad news about my dad. He turned himself in down at the VA for psych issues. Turns out he tried to kill himself the same night we all had dinner together." A wall of guilt fell upon Carl. He reached over and took Tara's hand in his. Guilt flooded his mind. He cautiously replied,

"Yeah, I could tell he was on edge. It was Nam. Saw something that maybe he shouldn't have seen there. When he got up to get some beers the other day, I unloaded his gun when he wasn't looking. Thought it was better that way. You know what I mean?" Tara then became very emotional and got up from the couch and held her face in hand. He stood up, and the two embraced. Somewhere in between the moment of gratitude and sadness there was a kiss involved. Unexpectedly, the two had become one.

8

The month of October was coming to an end in the five boroughs. The Ginko tree leaves were now turning an off shade of yellow, and people were starting to wear their wool coats again. All the street corner merchants were out hawking their hats, scarves and gloves. It was all of the usual stuff that had the emblematic NYC branding on it. It was cheap apparel for the busy tourists. As the seasons changed, so did the clothing, but the people were still exactly the same. They rudely hustled, pushing past the slow-moving tourists who stopped to take their pictures of everything an everywhere.

Sometimes with the backdrop of the Manhattan sky line, the many lives of the many people seemed like a movie script being played out, all while the casual observer watched from afar. And then, there was the artist who was up a 2a.m. working under a single table lamp, toiling away on something that was more important than sleep. A feminine dark figure watched him as he was immersed in his own private universe of creativity. Tara grew bored of his working so hard, got up out of bed and walked over to Carl's drafting table. She was listless and started running her fingers over his hardened body. Without speaking, her body was demanding his attention now. She leaned in closer to whisper then.

"Come back to bed love. I need you to keep me warm, baby." She then ran her hand down the inside of his leg. Carl's eyes suddenly got bigger. In the early morning hours, the two figures laid together and merged into one thought. As they engaged once more in their lovemaking, two small figures stood silently in the shadows, waiting for their next opportunity to take Carl away from this collectively mundane world.

PART III

Did you ever notice, bad things
always happen in threes?

It was 3:30a.m. in the borough of Brooklyn, New York. The heat island effect was now taking hold as July entered the calendar year. Some residents, who could afford to, escaped to the shoreline and traveled further up North to their vacation homes. Those who were less fortunate had to make due and just sweat-it-out. If you were smart, you would avoid the heat and brutal humidity of the NYC Transit System during the months of July and August. It smelled of both piss and body odor at every station. You could say this was part of the cities charm, but not if you lived there. This underground system also became the catch basin for all those who were unwanted and unseen.

During warm summer nights, some residents slept with their windows open. Most people, however, had their air conditioners going to escape the heat and noise happening on the streets below. On one of those warm nights, Carl was dreaming of swimming with a pod of sperm whales. The water was a crystal clear blue. Here he felt at home and less of a stranger to this water world than he did in his own. In the second part of the dream, he was standing in a vast desert of sand with nothing else around him. This place felt both foreign and vacant to him. Off into the distance, he could see four suns burning the landscape with their combined heat. Out of nowhere, a lone figure stepped out in front of him. He wore traditional desert garb and was covered from head to toe, so you could only see his steel blue eyes. Without saying a word, the man took his pointer finger and tapped Carl in the middle of the forehead. The touch sounded like a gunshot going off and he woke up to the sirens ringing on the street below. His heart was pounding after the shot went off, not being able to deduce what was reality and what was a dream.

Instead of looking out the window to see what was unfolding on the Brooklyn streets, he instead ran to his notebook. It was there that he rerecorded all the details of this visionary dream, but something else stood out to him. There were numbers in this dream too. They were: 45-454. But what did that mean? Were they coordinates, a mailbox number, a hidden date, or maybe... he wasn't sure. This dream was something more spiritual in feeling. As he continued to have experiences with the "phenomenon," his psychic gifts were emerging as well. One of the most prominent gifts was meeting his Spirit Guide, Carlos.

This guide, Carlos, was once a Mexican Shaman who used to walk the desert and had helped people with their death-rights when they were ready to make the transition into the afterlife. He explained to Carl that he didn't die the usual physical death but instead, walked out of this reality into the next one. Since meeting Carlos, his dreams had taken on a whole other dimension. The lines of reality were much more of a blur. He often questioned himself, as if his waking life was, in fact, really a dream. The multitudes of realities were never ending. The universe had gotten even bigger now, and at times, was more confusing to him. The dreams became the muse, and the more he learned, the less he felt that he understood. Carlos often said to him, "We can never understand it all. We must accept that which is in front of us and for everything else, there is simple faith."

The funny part of this all was how it came to be. For weeks, Carl had been talking to himself. This turned into a two way conversation at some point. There was a point when he thought he was answering himself back. But one day, the voice said, "Hello estupido, I'm talking to you! My name is Carlos. We are both the same person, for all things are ONE." This introduction was then followed shortly there after by an avalanche of questions from Carl. His curiosity went wild, and the universe just got a little bigger.

2

It was well into the upper 90's on the rooftop of Carl's apartment building. Both he and Willy, the buildings Superintendent were now keeping bees up there. The hope was to maybe sell the honey if the venture were to succeed. If not, it was at the very least something fun to try. Willy had asked Carl one day,

"So what the hell prompted you to have this idea? I never heard of anyone wanting to have bees in the city before, let alone get honey from a rooftop hive? You some kinda' hippie?" Carl laughed to himself and explained,

"It was a dream I had a long time ago when I was a kid. It was really weird too."

"Lots of shit is weird about you, Carl, if you don't mind me saying so."

"Yeah, I get that a lot... So about the dream. I was in a large round room with these enormous bees. They didn't feel any different than myself, like I was at home there. I could touch the honeycomb, and they didn't seem to mind. So after that, I always felt some sort of affinity toward bees. And of course, I like the honey too."

What Carl failed to mention to Willy was the loud machine noises that he heard in the bee room or the fact that this had taken place onboard a UFO. No, he wouldn't understand. He didn't think anyone would ever understand how abstract these experiences could be. Even now, they still periodically came and either made their presence known to him or took him onboard one of their ships. It didn't make a difference where he was living either. These visits always seemed to be either one of two things. There were the medical type of check-ups which involved implants or learning something new in the classrooms. The strangest part of the classrooms was how human they all were. They had imitated the human school rooms perfectly. This was so that it wouldn't jar you out of the altered state that they put you under while you were there.

The last time he had visited a classroom was a trip unto itself. The mechanics came and took him from his studio apartment. Next thing he knew, he was in the middle of a soccer field joining hands again with four other people. Next, they simultaneously crouched down together before being beamed up into the craft. The process was very loud, like a wind tunnel effect, and he felt as if he needed to hold his breath. The feeling was as if he were being held under water. It seemed familiar and he couldn't remember why?

Once onboard, he noted that this was another one of the classrooms. There was a traditional white board with a western style painting of a buffalo attached to it. After he noticed this, he was then shown another buffalo, except it looked more like a symbol for one. The translation was both literal and obvious at the same time. The experience ended with that. It somehow felt like the lesson was being repeated for him there. What really frustrated him about the ordeal was that he couldn't remember anyone's face. This was a common problem, unless it was an ET that he normally dealt with, like the Doctor one who managed his implants. Otherwise he didn't remember the faces. There was a dreamlike effect to this too. Sometimes, the faces he remembered were friendly and nice, while at other times they were utterly terrifying to him. The impulse of emotion was impossible for him to control. These experiences held next to seeing an actual ghost or apparition, were nothing in comparison. The level of fear was unlike anything else he would ever experience in his waking life.

Carl put the smoker down next to the hive after the bees appeared to be calming down. He was getting more comfortable with them now and was only wearing his mesh-covered hat to keep the bees off of his face. As usual, he first checked to make sure the queen was still there. She was marked with a purple dot on her back. He'd read about colony collapse disorder and was nervous the same thing would happen to his hive. If half your worker bees disappeared, you were in big trouble. Carlos was standing over Carl's shoulder observing his movements like a teacher does with one of their best students.

"All the best people are a little crazy, Carl. Now I want you to look at the structure of the honeycombs. There is no wasted space, just like a good artist; there are no wasted ideas. Notice their symmetry, too. It's intelligent design. Everything in the Universe contains this type of structuring, but it isn't always so obvious."

"So you're saying that I need to look at the building blocks of life, right?"

"Yes, something like that, amigo." And then Carlos leaned in closer to Carl. He blew into his ear, and a static noise filled his mind's eye. In a moment, he was no longer standing on the roof top. Carl was now floating out-of-body, suspended in outer space. The static noise was the actual sound of the void of space surrounding him. Looking down, he could see the Milky Way and the spiral that made up its natural form. In another quick movement he was observing the human DNA structure, which was also spinning in a similar spiral formation.

"Now do you see? Everything is moving in unison. The galaxy, the human DNA, even the fish in the ocean are moving with this synchronicity. It's the hand of God, Carl!"

"Hello, Carl! Earth to Carl! Tara was now on the rooftop with him. She snapped her fingers to break the glassy daze he was under. "You're talking to him again, aren't you?" He was totally entranced and hadn't noticed that Tara had come up onto the roof top with him. The present world, for a moment, had simply melted away. Tara was now standing directly in front of Carl.

"I thought I'd find you up here." Carl rolled his eyes feeling Tara was going to lecture him again.

"No, I wasn't avoiding you. I was just thinking about some story ideas for a new graphic novel that I wanted to write."

"And your notebook is where? Yeah, you should be at your drawing table in your studio." Carl smiled at Tara in recognition of being called out. "I know, I know... get off my ass woman."

Carlos was still standing close by and whispered to Carl, "She has secrets... The Universe is in movement again. Hold on."

Carl looked at Tara, who was still wearing her nurse scrubs. The man in Carl was sort of turned on by seeing her in uniform. He moved in closer to kiss her hello, but she seemed sort of cold and indifferent to his gesture. This made him suddenly nervous.

"So, what's up?" It was obvious by her body language that she was holding something back. Her eyes were avoiding him now.

"Well, a couple things, I guess. First thing: my position was eliminated at the hospital, only God knows why." Then there was a long pause. Carl raised his eyebrows in anticipation. "And the second thing, um, I'm, um pregnant." Carl became wide eyed.

"Come again?"

"Yep, I've been waiting a while to see. You know I've had certain issues in the past, so I didn't want to jump the gun and say so." Carl had made a mental note to himself several weeks ago when Tara had stopped smoking and drinking. But he kept his mouth shut about it. Carl took a deep breath to center himself before speaking.

"I'm happy, Tara, It's okay. This is a good thing. Not the job part, but the baby part is. Come here, let me at least hold you. You look so nervous. I promise, it will be okay."

As the two lovers embraced, Tara mentioned the fact that the doctor had told her she wasn't capable of getting pregnant, and jokingly said, "Unless by some act of God." And here it was, the world was changing. There was going to be a little more pressure on Carl to support his family. Today, the boy finally became a man.

3

It was around 3a.m. again, when Carl woke up from another lucid dream. There was an anxiety from it too. His jaw was sore from grinding his teeth. He just laid there for a while trying to fall back asleep. Things started to cross his mind: Tara being pregnant, one less paycheck coming in, his freelance jobs and deadlines for his graphic novel.

The story had been percolating in the back of his mind for many weeks now. This always seemed to happen too. He would be working on one project and get a sudden burst of creativity for another story right away. It was hard to stay on track sometimes. Carl had to remind himself; take it moment by moment and situation by situation. One story at a time, he would often tell himself. It was hard to fight the muse however. The universe kept throwing ideas at him from all different directions. If it wasn't a dream, then it was Carlos, and if it wasn't Smitty, then it was Barry's war stories. It was suffocating at times. The world was built on these creative possibilities.

Carl finally gave in, got up and went to work. He made his way to the kitchen to make a pot of coffee. Then he quietly went to his drawing board, trying not to wake Tara up, again. He sat before his table, with just a table light on. The title of his graphic novel was to be "Death House Whisper."

Notes: The protagonist is John Farmer, and it's 1954. His wife has just died, making him a widow. It is just him and his dog Bullet living on the farm. Every dog he has is named "Bullet." John believes it's the same soul coming back to him each time he gets a new dog. The farm is only 43 acres after some of the land was sold off to pay the bills. The farm is located in the Hudson Valley. Farmer makes boot-leg whiskey, and people stop by to buy some from time to time. He generally likes to keep to himself, except for his friend Preacher, who is his drinking buddy. On the farm there is an area that he does not touch. It is a Native American burial ground. Farmer feels it's his responsibility to look after this place. It means so much to him that he buries his wife there. The farm has a history of strange phenomenon happening. Some examples are: ghosts, things disappearing, energy vortexes that cause visions, etc. The highlight of the story is John waking up to his dog being trapped in the closet. He has no idea how this happened? Out in the yard where he dumps his coal ash, a hole in the earth has opened up. This hole is a vortex that leads back into his closet. To prove this theory is correct he tricks Preacher into looking down the hole and pushes him in. Next, he runs back to the house and opens the closet door to let him back in. History: The Hudson Valley has a history of UFO sightings and abductions. This will add to the story line, too. At the end of the story, John and Preacher are sitting around a fire singing the Moon Shiners song: Lyrics came from Smitty and Irv while fishing the Long Island Sound.

"Moon Shiners Song"

Get your copper kettle
get your copper coil
Fill it with good sour mash
and you'll no longer toil

Make your fire's of hickory
Of hickory, ash and oak
don't burn no green, no rotten wood
they'll catch you by your smoke

My daddy made corn whiskey
my grand daddy made it too…
and we ain't paid no whiskey tax since 1792

*Chorus: Sit beneath the juniper while the moon shines bright
and watch the moon shine so bright
and watch the jugs filling in the pale moon light*

The Death House Whisper
by Carl Smith

The off-white color of the plaster ceiling was accentuated by brown water stains faded by the hands of time. No two marks were the same, and there were ovals, circles and holes exposing the attic's moldy stained insulation. This old farm house has many stains. Some from births, some from deaths and others from the unholy whisper of ghosts.

Before you turn to the left and put your hand on the newel post, look down at your feet. Take one step back from the carpet; the blood stain is still there. No amount of cleaning would ever wash it away. Time will not forget.

It was the month of October in the year of our Lord 1931, and autumn was baring its teeth down on the tiny town of Roxbury. No, it wasn't a dark cloud as they like to say, but rather a shadow shaped like the cloak of evil.

They say it was after the first frost that came late in the month. On one sorrowful day, a farm laborer from over at Thompson's orchard had to be put down like a dog gone astray. Something unholy came over him there. They say there was a look in his eyes after he was confronted in the barn by his boss. It was said that he became possessed by an unspeakable evil.

Yes, I remember the day like it was yesterday. I said, "Turn around boy, I'm talking to you!" But as he did, I swear his eyes were red like the Devil himself. That son of bitch growled like a dog at me."

Some figure next to the hey bales then moved, and I looked past him to see what it was. Over in the corner was this unspeakable creature. It kinda looked like a man and a goat at the same time. Its skin had sparse patches of hair and was an oily gray color. It was sitting on its hackles, alone in the shadow of the hay bales. A chill went up my spine. I said, "Who goes there!" It too spoke in an unholy voice. I'll never forget what it said.

"I is Slanx." It called itself Slanx? After it spoke, there was the smell of sulfur in the air. The smell of death I tell you.

God as my witness, I stepped back in fear for my own, and almost tripped over my own two feet. The thing disappeared before my eyes in that moment. I made the sign of the cross, and just as I did Jake pushed on past me like a mad dog set loose from the gates of Hell. Something dark came over him. It possessed him somehow."

You know, some men are weak that way. They ain't got no belief in God and the like. Probably never said one prayer in all his days neither. Maybe he's the son of whore. Either way, I got shoved off to the side. By the time I righted myself, I spotted him running across the field, He was headed over toward the Smith's farm. I feared for their young daughters just then.

I ran out of the barn fearing the worst. Soon as I saw Preacher, I said, "Get your shotgun, something wicked this way comes." On the way out of the barn, I had picked up an old hickory pick-ax handle for myself. Before we gave chase, we called on old Levy Freeman to join us.

He's bigger than both of us combined. Lord, he's a big black man.

The three of us came together like one. We gave chase across the old pumpkin patch and up through the apple orchard from there. After the apple trees there was a hedge wood that stood in front of us, a wall of thorn. There's no telling how Jake made it through this hedge. We decided it was best to double back and come back up the other side of the grove. There was no way we were passing through the blackberry thorns.

By the time we came upon the Smith's place, we could here a young woman's scream before we even made it to the front porch. Freeman kicked in the door and nearly took it off its hinges. There in front of us was one of the young girls on the floor. She was knocked out cold and another was in the clutches of Jake. He stood over her at the staircase that led up to the second floor. I could clearly see his hand was on her throat too.

Levy moved past us to help the young girl who was knocked out. Like an angel, he held her in his arms and patted her on the cheek trying to get her to wake up.

Then Jake was looking back at us. He growled, and I swear to Christ, his eyes were red like a midnight fire. The strangest thing happened as I locked eyes with him. A tall shadow then moved across the wall behind him. The smell of sulfur came back to me, and then I knew that death was here. I heard another voice in the room with us. It said,

"Do it. Kill her now! She is ours to take."

Instinct took over, and I stepped up to him with my ax handle and swung my hardest. This momentarily knocked him down. I quickly realized that this was no longer a man I was facing. It was evil incarnate.

So I looked to Preacher and yelled, "Shoot God damn it. Shoot that bastard!" He pulled the triggers, unleashing both barrels. The sound of two twelve gauge shots going off in a confined space made me lose hearing for a bit. My ears still ring to this day. But in the eyes of God, we did what had to be done."

There it sits, the Smith's old farm house. It has been vacant ever since that time evil came to Roxbury, our small town in the Hudson. People know about this event, but it's an unsaid rule that we don't talk about it. Some even say that they've seen shadows moving in that house still to this day. As for me, I walk on the right side of the Lord. I say thanks every day for this life I got. The site of such evil will forever haunt me. Then Eddy looked over at Preacher.

"Say Preacher, is all that evil business true, or is old Danny pulling my leg? I don't believe in no devil business." Then Preacher leaned in real close to him.

"There are some things in this world that man simply can't explain. I would never have thought any of this kind of thing to be true, but there I was. I held that young child in my arms and tried to get her to come around. Her eyes opened. Soon as they did, they rolled into the back of her head. She died in my arms. I wept like she was my own child. It still haunts me to this day."

-THE END

At 5a.m. the phone rang startling Carl and finally waking up Tara. Carl picked up the phone, and the women on the other line says,

"Hi this is nurse Judy from Saint Raphael Hospital in New Haven. Is this Carl Smith?"

"Yes, yes it is."

"I'm calling on behalf of your mother, and I see that you are her emergency contact. I need to inform you that she's had a stoke. She's stable now and under our care" Carl gripped the edge of his writing desk in anger.

"Can I ask, how bad is it?"

"Well, there will be some rehab involved. There will also be some issues with paralysis from the stroke. She will need to be put into a rehab unit for a while."

"But she's going to make it, right?"

"Yes, of course. But you will need to speak with her doctor and get the rest of the details. When will you be stopping in?"

"I'll get there by tomorrow afternoon, the latest."

"Okay, thanks, Carl." The call ended there and Carl quickly turned to see if Tara was fully awake yet. He reached out and gently touched her side.

"Hey, are you awake?"

"Yes, I am now..."

"So you heard at least half of the conversation then?"

"Yes, a little, but fill me in on the rest. What's this all about? Is your mother okay?" Then Carlos interrupted Carl's thoughts and said, "Bad things happen in three's Carl. Watch out." Carl tripped over his tongue losing his train of thought. Tara rolled her eyes and asked again.

"Carl, is your mother okay?"

"Well, the nurse said she had a stroke and is going to need to be put in rehab."

"I'm so sorry, Carl..."

"Yeah, me too."

After the "bad news," both Carl and Tara sat down for breakfast. They spoke for quite some time trying to figure out what was the best course of action. Tara was pretty much onboard with whatever Carl wanted to do. She was out of a job collecting unemployment now. So after a couple cups of coffee and some Jewish bagels from the local bakery, it was decided that they would rent a car and drive up to Connecticut. Once there, they would stay at Carl's mom's house for a few weeks. They planned on making regular trips to New Haven to visit his mother. For Tara, she was excited just to hang out on Horseshoe Beach and read her trashy romance novels. Carl would often pick them up, shake his head and ask her, "Why do you read this stuff?" Then she would taunt him back by saying, "You could learn a thing or two from those books, Carl Smith."

They set off around 10a.m. to avoid the rush hour traffic. Carl remarked about how weird it was to have a car to drive around whenever they wanted. The city life versus the suburban life was like two totally different universes. Tara noted that each time they took a trip up to see Carl's mom, she would need to decompress from the drama of the city. Even sleeping without the noise was a challenge for them. After growing up in the city, the hustle and bustle became like a white noise. It was just always there, like a ringing in your ears that you got used to.

After spending a couple hours on Route 91 North, they made it to the Quinnipiac Bridge. This joined New Haven to the small bedroom town of Branford. The traffic and routing of the "Q" was the ire of all the local residents too. As they moved through the traffic, Tara suddenly asked, "What the hell is that smell, Carl?" He went on to explain how they unloaded oil at this port. You didn't always get hit by it, but when you did, it was freaking nasty. Didn't matter if your car windows were up or down.

Just as they were cresting the bridge, traffic had come to an abrupt stop for roadwork. Carl put on his blinker, but before he could change lanes, they were slammed from behind by another car. This folded up their rentals trunk like an accordion. As a result, both Carl and Tara got whiplash and had a follow up trip to the ER to get checked out. Carl's main concern was Tara's baby. This was all he could think about. He had jumped out of the car and started cursing out the guy who had hit them. The incident came close to blows just before an off-duty cop had stepped in to help out.

4

After many long hours spent in the emergency room, both Carl and Tara finally made it back to Smitty's house. Today, nothing had gone as planned and because of the accident, Tara had a follow-up with the OBGYN in a couple days to make sure everything was okay with the baby. She was hesitant, but Carl insisted that she do what's best for the baby. In the back of his mind, he had envisioned himself as a father now, and unlike his father, he would be there for his kid. Of that he was certain.

As they made there way into the kitchen looking for something to eat, Tara noticed that Susan had left a yellow envelope on the table with Carl's name on it. She quickly pointed it out to him, and he downplayed it and said he'd open it later. She found his behavior peculiar and watched him going through the fridge looking for a beer. Feeling impatient, she finally asked,

"Are you going to open that envelope or what?" Carl was acting totally indifferent to her question.

"Maybe later when I have had a chance to collect my thoughts" Tara gritted her teeth.

"Come on, open it, please." Tara was obviously annoyed now.

"No, it's personal. I'll take care of it later. Don't worry."

"Fine, be that way. Please fix us something to eat while you are at it." She finally gave up and walked out of the kitchen to go settle in and unpack.

After dinner, Tara took a warm bath and afterwords lied in bed with ice on her sore neck. Carl retreated to Smitty's library with a beer and a few pain killers. Once there, he settled in like usual and took out his notebooks and sketch pads. He called this his "pop up studio." Carl sat back in the wooden office chair and looked around the room. There were so many memories here. -The books, record player, butter scotch candies and the secret wall compartment. All of these things were left as is by his mother. She knew how special this room was to Carl and left it like a memorial to her late father.

Carl was suddenly startled when Tara entered the room, catching him off guard. Tara gave him a smile and said, "Don't worry, love. I'll be okay." Carl had reservations. He'd always been a glass half empty kind of guy. Tara came and sat across from him still in her bathrobe.

"You look like the big boss sitting behind that desk, ya know? What trouble are you up to in here anyway?"

Nothing much, just getting my stuff ready for work. I still have that freelance job I need to get finished by next week. The deadline is hanging over me like a stone, and I hate it."

"One step at a time, Carl. Worry about your mom first, then work."

"Yeah, I know..." Changing the subject abruptly he said,

"Oh, did I ever show you the hidden compartment in here?" Tara's eyes widened all of a sudden, as she perked up and became very interested all of a sudden.

"No, please show me... I love that kind of stuff." Carl then got up and walked over to the one wall covered in floral wallpaper. Slowly he ran his hand down low on it until he felt a seam. Tara's eyes were fixed upon him now. Once he reached the seam, he gave the wall a gentle push, and the panel popped off to reveal a hidden alcove. Carl got down on his hands and knees and stuck his head in while he looked around. Tara finally said,

"Hey, let me have a look!" Carl was baiting her, and she didn't see it coming. Tara then got down on all fours and stuck her head in.

"What's this little box doing in here?" She snatched it up and turned to Carl who was holding back a smile.

"I don't know. Why don't you open it and see. It could be a treasure." Tara opened the box, and her eyes lit up. Their was a ring signifying that their relationship was now at another level. This is what she had secretly been hoping for.

"You son of a bitch! You got me, and the answer is yes! I love you. Come here and kiss me, you jerk. This was in the envelope, wasn't it?" Carl laughed and shook his head yes.

"Oh, you got me good... and I got a little treasure for you too... Lets go in the other room, shall we." Carl was flushed with excitement of what Tara was implying just then. "I'm right behind you baby."

Carl and Tara eventually fell asleep around 11:00. It had been an exhausting day, and they dozed off within seconds of hitting the pillow. The night air was cool, and they had left the windows wide open with just the ceiling fan on. Around 2a.m. the bedroom lit up like there was lighting flashing outside, yet everything remained completely still. A static filled the air, and they were still sound asleep.

The floorboard squeaked as if someone were walking into their room. Carl opened one eye, but no one was there. He assumed it was his imagination, or was it? The floor squeaked again, and he saw two short thin figures standing over him. Suddenly he felt paralyzed both physically and mentally. One of the beings was holding a black glass orb that refracted the light in the room. The other had a long cylindrical wand that looked as if it were made from stainless steel. The last thing he remembered was it saying, "Sleep." Everything went black.

The newly-engaged couple slept in late the next morning. They were supposed to drive into New Haven after lunch to see Carl's mom. Again, things didn't go as planned. Carl woke up to Tara patting his side. She seemed frantic and yelled out his name.

"Carl, wake up! Wake the fuck up! Something is wrong."

"What? What's wrong?"

"I don't feel right. My stomach hurts. Something ain't right. Get up! We're going to the doctor, now! And as Tara stood up, she realized that she was bleeding from her vagina. Quickly she looked down and then up at Carl and screamed out.

"Fuck! No, no, no, this ain't right."

Not wasting a second, Carl told her to take a quick shower and then he would drive her to the OBGYN right away. Carl called while she was still cleaning up and said it was "an emergency appointment."

When the couple arrived to the doctor's office, Tara quickly filled out the paperwork and rushed it over to the receptionist. Twice she reminded the woman that it was an emergency appointment. After fifteen minutes, they were finally called into the office. The usual procedure ensued. There was the paper gown, cold lube, probing, followed up by an ultrasound.

The woman who was the OB asked the usual questions. She wanted to know all about her food intake, activity level, stress and so on. As she held the wand up to her stomach, she began to have a very puzzled look on her face.

"You took a pregnancy test and visited your OBGYN, right?"

"Yes I did, after I took a home pregnancy test too."

"And how far along are you?"

"Like only a couple months. Why?"

"And you, sir, are the father, correct?"

"Yes, yes I am."

"Okay then. Well you must have miscarried. I'm sorry to say this, but there is no child here any longer. Did you notice anything odd after going the bathroom? Like a bloody discharge? Tara began to sob and Carl reached out to hold her hand. Wiping away the tears Tara said,

"No, I didn't see anything irregular. Only thing that happened was the car accident yesterday. I got whiplash and went to the Emergency Room with Carl afterwords."

Forty minutes later, both Carl and Tara left the doctor's office and were feeling both helpless and low now. They couldn't imagine how this had happened. There didn't seem to be any answers from the doctor either. The terms of this situation left them with a great deal of uncertainty.

When they got back to the house, Tara went upstairs and drew a hot bath for herself. She sat in warm water wiping away the tears for the next hour. Carl eventually knocked on the door and asked if he could come in. Tara reluctantly said "yes." He slowly came in handing her a glass of wine and sat on the toilet looking down at the pink bath mat under his feet. Trying not to make eye contact he said,

"I'm so sorry, love."

"Yeah, I know. Me too. Is there a dark cloud hanging over us or what?"

"Kinda feels like that lately. It's like one thing after another, after another. First it was my mom, then the car accident, and now this. Where does it end?"

"Carl, I lost my baby. What the fuck is going on? It was a brief miracle that got taken away from me. I wasn't supposed to be able to get pregnant. It's like God's punishing me or something." Tara then put her head on her knees as if she were trying to curl up and disappear.

"Please don't punish yourself. It's not your fault Tara. I love you babe. I'm here for you. We got each other. Don't forget that."

5

The days that followed the missing baby incident were only a little better. For now both Carl and Tara would settle into a routine at the house. Carl would stay up late working on his art projects. He even started drawing up storyboards for "The Light of Darkness." The freelance job was finished now too. The emotional pain all got channeled into his work. Tara often sat in the library with him and read while he worked long hours. The mornings were spent traveling into New Haven to visit Carl's mom. She had been overjoyed that they were now engaged. Susan was also working with a speech therapist now to help her speak correctly again. The side of her face had some droopiness from the stroke. Despite all that had happened, the young couple did their best to persevere. For hours, Carl would hold Tara, spooning in bed trying to give her some comfort from the pain.

One afternoon, after Tara and Carl had come back from the lawyer's office, Carl felt frustrated by all the car accident business and decided to do some drawing. He needed to take his mind off of things. Tara was still feeling very vulnerable and quietly joined him in the library. Having run out of things to read, she started going through Smitty's books looking for something interesting to read. She came across a small hand bound book titled "The Thinking Stones." Curious, she sat down on the floor in front of the bookcase reading it. It was a quick read, and she broke the silence by asking Carl about this strange story.

"Hey, Carl. You ever read this book called "The Thinking Stones?"

"No, why?" She held it up in the air for him to see.

"This is right up your alley with it being totally weird."

"Oh?"

"Yeah, let me read it to you. It's short."

"Sure, go ahead..." As Tara sat there reading aloud to Carl for the next ten minutes, Carl stopped what he was doing to listen better. He was very intrigued. The book was so small he had never noticed it there. He then asked,

"So who's the author?" Tara looked up at him.

"It doesn't have one. Do you think Smitty wrote it?"

"I'm not sure. Anything is possible with the old man. He was full of secrets."

"Yeah, just like his grandson, right?" Carl frowned and stuck his tongue out at her. She was right about that. Tara felt that he was always hiding something from her, and she was well aware of his visits from "THEM." You don't sleep with someone that experiences the "Phenomenon" and not think that it isn't somehow affecting you too. Carl had even showed her the notes and photos from Smitty. Reluctantly, she became a believer after seeing one of "THEM" in the studio. She had no choice but to believe then.

The baby trauma was still weighing on her mind. She tried to put on a good face when she was around Carl; inside she was very depressed. The grief was standing on her heart.

Later that evening Carl was up at around midnight still working on his storyboards. Taking a break, he decided to take another look at "The Thinking Stones." He thought to himself, "Maybe Smitty did write this, but why? Was it "THEM" that had given him the story or perhaps asked him to write it?" Carlos his guide then added his two cents.

"The truth always comes out somewhere, Carl. Only problem, is that you don't know where it comes out and for who."

Carl sat there sucking down a beer and thumbing through the book, rereading it again and again. On the second read, a light went off in his head. He had finally made the connection. "Yes, that's it," he thought. It was the man in my dream, the desert man. Putting down the book, he went into the bedroom and woke Tara up to tell her that he made the connection. She was half asleep listening to him explain how the desert man had shown up in his dream last week. He was jumping around crazy like he'd discovered gold. Tara just laid there with one eye open and finally said,

"You're crazy. You know that, right? No more beer for you. Go to bed. I mean it!"

Later on, Carl slipped into bed around 1a.m. and finally dozed off. He always felt excited when he managed to connect the dots. It was like the spirit world was winking back at him. As he nodded off, Carlos whispered in his ear, "We are all One, Carl. It's all One."

At 4a.m., Carl was jolted awake by Tara screaming in her sleep. She was having a horrible nightmare. Now fully awake, Carl clearly heard her say,

"No! You can't have my baby. It's mine. No, please don't take my baby!" After that, Carl gently shook her until she finally woke up. She was inconsolable. Wiping her eyes, she looked at Carl.

"It was "THEM"! They took my baby Carl. It was "THEM." She kept crying as Carl held her in his arms trying to give her some comfort. In the moment, he didn't want to press her for the details, but he believed her nonetheless. And in that moment, he also felt very guilty for not mentioning that They came to his bedside that night too. It felt like it was his fault somehow. He was sure of it.

The next morning he let Tara sleep in while he got up and took care of things around the house. Tara finally emerged from the bedroom around 11:00. It was plain to see that she was still very upset from her dream, if that was in fact what it was. Carl sat across from her at the kitchen table while she silently sipped at her coffee. Finally he broke the silence and asked,

"Can I make you some eggs and toast for breakfast?" Still not speaking, she simply nodded "yes." Ten minutes later Carl put a plate in front of her. All she did was just push the food around in a circle. She was sitting there, but her mind was somewhere else.

"You wanna tell me about it?"

"Talk about what Carl? How the fucking little spacemen hijacked me and took our fucking baby. No, not really." Her words cut to the bone.

Carl sat back in his chair, crossed his arms and bit his lip. He was nervous, really nervous. He knew full well how these things affected people. It affected him too, as he had flashbacks to his childhood. This wasn't something you just got over. No, this type of event left a permanent scar. It walked with you like a shadow, even on the brightest of days. Once you knew, there was no way of not knowing. The reality bubble was popped. The "phenomenon" watched you. It toyed with you. It listened to your every word. Dimensions of reality collapsed in on them selves, an innocence lost.

Carl, however, sometimes felt lucky that he had had the experiences that he did, even if others would never understand. It was like something woke up inside of him. The world was much bigger now. They inspired him, and through his artistic lens, there were a thousand more colors to play with. Secretly it made him feel very special and unique, though he never told anybody that. And overall, it gave his life more purpose and meaning.

6

On Saturday morning both Carl and Tara sat out on the beach over looking Long Island Sound. Kids played at the waters edge digging big holes in the sand. Carl watched people sunning themselves out on the wooden raft of Horseshoe beach. There were some teenage boys out on the rock-face using the old diving board too. Sitting there he felt nostalgic, like he were still an innocent boy playing without the weight of the world on his shoulders. It was then that he thought to himself how lucky people are for not having to know what he did. How easy their lives must be. Living small, simple lives in a little world.

Tara sat there silently reading her trashy romance novel. On the cover was a bare chested man with huge pecks holding a woman with a rose. Carl looked over at her not saying a word. The look on her face said don't talk to me. She was totally engrossed. The nightmare that Tara had was eating away at Carl. He felt responsible somehow. "How could this have happened?" he thought. "Were they being evil or good? How did they justify these actions? Was there malice in their intention?" He kept mulling it over and over in his mind. He couldn't think of any explanation. Human logic verse E.T. logic. It was all lost in translation.

Carl took a quick swim to cool off and came back to lay down on his beach towel. Feeling mentally exhausted, he laid back with his baseball cap over his face and fell asleep and very quickly fell into a dream. High over the Earth he could see the East Coast and the outline of Florida. Then he was standing at the shoreline while a tidal wave swept over the whole coastline. Nothing was left; no one had lived. Frightened, he jerked and sat up straight. Tara looked over at him raising an eyebrow.

"You okay?

"Yeah, I dozed off and had a messed up dream."

"About THEM?"

"No, I was looking down at the East coast of Florida, then I was at beach level. Next thing I know a huge tsunami comes crashing over everything and everyone. There were no survivors! No one below 250 feet survives. So much death!"

"That's really messed up, Carl. You gonna be one of those "New Age Prophets" now or something? Should we get a dooms day cult started for you?"

"Ha ha ha, very funny. No, but this dream seemed so real!"

"Notebook, Carl. Write it in your notebook."

"It's at the house."

"So, go get it..."

"Fine, I'll be back in fifteen."

Back at the house, Carl noticed that the light on the answering machine was blinking. It was Willy. He had called twice, and the first message was garbled. On the second message he could tell that something was wrong. He mentioned a fire in the building. Carl got a huge knot in his stomach. Panic set over him. Frantic, he called Willy back.

"Hey Willy. It's Carl."

"Oh, thanks for finally calling me back." There was sarcasm in his voice.

"So what happened? A fire?"

"Yeah, a fire in unit 12B, that fat guy Stu Farrenstein. You know him right?"

"Seen him around, never really talked to him. Why?"

"So get this. The guy spontaneously combusted. Only his body burned, nothing else. Should have heard the fire rescue guys talking afterwords. They ain't never seen nothing like it. Then there were detectives asking the other tenants questions, lots... of... questions... Really weird shit, huh?"

"So it was just unit 12B then?"

"Yeah, nothing else. Like and episode on the "The Twilight Zone." Soon as I heard this, I'm like oh man I gotta call Carl, knowing how freaking weird you are. Ha hah ha."

"Thanks for calling, Willy, I gotta run. Tara is at the beach alone. Really, I gotta get back to her."

"Wait, wait, wait, one more thing. There were these two guys who came around asking for you the other day. They were dressed in black suits with dark sunglasses, like secret service type of guys. Government spooks maybe?"

"Seriously? Fuck! Hey do me a huge favor and go into my studio. Walk to the far right corner. There's an old antique steamer chest. Take that and lock it up in the basement storage. Will yah?"

"Dare I even ask what's in it?"

"Not if you don't want to get into some deep shit."

"I'll lock it up for you tonight. You owe me some beer too, weirdo."

"Thanks, man." The call ended there but Carl's mind was awash in theories about what the men in black might have wanted. He considered the fact that maybe he leaked out too many facts about UFO's from Smitty's notes and ended up on the Fed's radar. There were so many possibilities here. It was time to lay low.

Carl finally made it back to the beach about an hour later. Tara looked up at him.

"You get lost or something? I was wondering if you weren't gonna come back."

"No, I had to call Willy back, there was a fire in the building." Tara's eyes got wide.

"Shit, is our stuff okay?"

"Yeah, it's fine. It was in apartment 12B. You know the pasty Jewish guy that eyes you at the mailbox sometimes?"

"Yeah, I know the one. He's a pervert. A total creeper man."

"So get this, he spontaneously combusted!"

"Carl, you know that shit ain't real. Come on?"

"No, I'm serious, up in flames, nothing else was burned, just him. Poof!"

"Come on! You're pulling my leg."

"Willy heard the fire rescue guys talking. He asked them, and they told him the whole story. Then there were "special investigators" there and everything. Oh, and totally unrelated, two government type guys stopped by looking for me at the studio, Willy said."

"Carl William Smith, I told you don't be fucking with this secret alien stuff too much!" Tara looked really pissed and concerned at the same time. "So whatcha going to do?"

"We'll make this an extended vacation, like for the summer. Mom won't care. Oh, and Willy's gonna hide my shit in the basement and lock it up. Nothing to worry about. It will blow over, trust me." Tara made a sour face at Carl and looked away.

"Feels like I'm engaged to someone from the X-files. You're fucking killing me, Carl."

7

It was 90 degrees Monday. There were heavy clouds overhead but no promise of rain for the coastline. An offshore breeze coming in from the Atlantic made the heat somewhat bearable. The usual faces were at Horseshoe beach. Kids played in the water and were throwing the clear jellyfish at each other. One kid got hit in the eye and let out a loud scream which prompted an adult to reprimand them.

Carl and Tara arrived in the afternoon with lunch. They sat there quietly eating their food until Carl pulled out a stack of paper and began reading as he ate his sandwich. Tara raised an eyebrow wondering what he was working on now.

"Was that what I heard you printing out late last night, Carl?"

"Yes, yes it was. Thought you were asleep, sorry."

"What are you working on now; dare I ask?"

"These are my notes from my experiences. I'm going to make it into a book someday."

"And what are you going to call this book?"

"Star-Seed Spiritual Mechanics, I think." Tara made another face like this was trouble.

"Okay, give it here. I'm gonna read this. You need the boss's approval first." Reluctantly, Carl handed over his paperwork. He seemed embarrassed that she was reading his stuff. Normally she wasn't interested in his comic book or spirit stories. It felt like he was in school having to report to the principal.

Carl's Book Notes:

STAR-SEED SPIRITUAL MECHANICS

FORWARD:

It's 6a.m. in the state of Connecticut where I live, and I've just been woken up by my neighbors dog, who is on her usual morning pee schedule. The dream I was just having before I woke up was a message from my Spirit Guides, "to finish reading the book I started reading over a year ago." Titled: "The New Human." It was just so I could start writing this one. And yes, I've agreed to write another book for THEM… Who is THEM? They, of course, are the E.T.s, the Extra Terrestrials. The ones who have somehow managed to impregnate their will and influence into every single writing project that I've ever worked on. With regards to my Spirit Guides, yes, some of them are in fact E.T.'s, and the others are more earthly. Then some are animals, and some are even Angels.

This menagerie of beings who are assisting me, given the current head count, is about twenty eight. That's at least what they've told me. It's to be them, in part, who help drive this book to where it needs to go. We are to be comrades in this endeavor. Both you and I are to be the students, together, as one. Yes, I want to learn just as much as you do, and I'm delighted that you are here with me right now in this very moment as we move forward.

The impetus for starting this project was a problem that I have. That problem is my "wall." Each of us who are on our own spiritual journey has, had to at various points, overcome spiritual obstacles before we are able to move forward and graduate to the next level. I thought it would be nice to take you along for the journey, too. I'm also going to give you the very basic tools to living as a spiritual person in this 3D world. We shall break it down for dissection. At least that is my intention. We may go out into a crazy no man's land if I don't stay focused. So you'll have to stop me if I get caught up in a tangent.

The wall I'm now facing is for not having a complete understanding of who all my Spirit Guides are. The reason I'm now facing this wall is that I've become a little stuck in my own personal development, not looking at the bigger picture, which is why you and I are going back to school to learn and review all the basic Mechanics which makes up our spiritual being. The goal is to have all my friends on the other side of the veil working in full support of me, so that I may better complete my mission here, as a Star-Seed. You didn't think I was actually from this planet, did you? No, I'm just visiting, mind you it's been a very, very long visit this time. But still, I'm just passing through, as a soul. I suspect the same is true for you as well.

There are lots of you Star-Seeds who are in the same boat as you and I this time around. The question is not who *we are, but what we do with it, that really matters. Chances are you feel the spiritual itch too and have started searching for your own purpose here. This mission of the Star-Seed may make everything else seem just like background noise, with regards to its importance. So let's scratch that itch!*

Introduction:

It is Wednesday, July 26th, the day after my girlfriend's birthday. Wednesday usually signifies that we are getting over the metaphorical hump in the work week. However, in the year of 20-something, this is not so. In fact, it is a year of heavy chains, strife, protests, political rebellion, human trafficking, wild fires and endless tropical storms. This year, is a year of confabulation and tribulation of all our maligned selves bottled up with a carbonation ready to blow its top. A biblical year. A God help us all kind of year. A "what the fuck?" kind of year.

The only good thing in this year is that we are all forced to deal with each other, to deal with each other once and for all. As we are all cooped up and locked down into our fears, there is a hope that we will gain a truer introspection of self. Today, if you were to turn on the television you would be both confused and nauseated at each and every human character trait. The flaw and identity problem needing its own special spotlight. It seems that we, the selfish humans, are utterly obsessed with feeling both special and separate from all our fellow humans.

The tides of strife are well orchestrated by the Elite Oligarchy, same as it ever was, with one exception. The internet of things. The world is now digitally connected in every possible way. You can call your refrigerator on the phone and see if you need more eggs, milk and cheese. In this new world of information, people now know the world's news within a matter of minutes. What is even more amazing is that both you and I are now the un-sponsored field reporters to these events. We are beating back all the newspapers and television networks with our self reporting before they can catch a breath of what is happening. To-this-point, people are now very important. We can tell a story, as only we are seeing it. People now hold the power to both share and distort the truth with the advent of the internet and cell phones. What power we have been given!

Identity, our identifier. What are we in this world being swallowed up by information? We are drunk on information. This is only if it comes in tiny little thirty second sound bites. Humans you see, like the thirty second film clip, the one where they don't even have to read. Reading? Each year, paper book sales dwindle more and more, so forget about getting rich from selling your next novel. The new money, so it seems, is in cute cat videos. Humans… what the Fuck! It's very obvious when someone isn't well-read in these times, especially when you speak with someone, and their vocabulary is lacking. You could be at the top of your class with straight A's in 20-something but sound like a fast-food attendant when you open your mouth. Yes, that is what is happening in our high-tech world of zero degree attention spans. We are, in essence, dumbing down our society in epic proportions. A very sad truth.

Getting back to my Wednesday, and why not. The world, maybe if we are lucky, is just starting to wake up within certain circles of people and in short order realizing things are not okay. People are getting both richer and poorer, all while the extreme weather is slapping us in the face. Some people are finally hearing the pop from having cranial-rectal-inversion. They are coming to the same realization, through this quick exchange of information, that we are in fact kind of sick and depressed as a society. But why? Maybe it's too much money and time on our hands. The Devil's workshop. Maybe it's a side effect of going to work for fifty hours a week and then coming home and staring at our tiny computer screens for hours on end. This is all while drinking florescent green energy drinks and ignoring our romantic partners at the same time. How else do you explain cute cat videos? Not that I've got anything against cats.

The world, more than ever, needs these new insta-reporters, especially the Star-Seed ones. It can be by whatever medium they so choose to exchange information. People want to be both distracted and entertained simultaneously when they get the news in this day in age.

The lowly paperback book may get pushed aside for the more popular online videos, but I don't count them out. The books are not dead yet. Books don't run out of batteries and are never lost to digital recalls. My bookshelf is my library, and no one can touch or take that away from me. For some greater introspection on the matter, please read Fahrenheit 451 by Ray Bradbury. This dystopian reality may come true if we're not careful. And remember, it wasn't that long ago when the Nazi's were burning books. Hold onto your books people!

In a connected world, the small, select, niche groups of people who are waking up can have lots in common with each other or nothing at all. They may seem to either stand out in a crowd, or may choose to totally blend in. They may also be overtly outspoken or maybe total wallflowers. People who are starting to "wake up" are coming from all walks of life and from all socioeconomic groups as well. So with that all being said, what ties them all together, if the identifier is so annoyingly obtuse?

The thing that is tying a lot of people together may seem very foreign and abstract to a lot of people but not to us Star-Seeds. You may walk past each other in the streets, make eye contact, smile, then keep walking. Both parties sensed and felt it, right? You've also stood next to that one person in line and felt as if you've known him/her your entire life. No, I'm not talking about love and soulmates. What I'm talking about here, is your galactic thread, your Star-Seed origin. It's the hidden DNA that you are all sharing and feeling on the quantum mainframe of our universal spiritual backbone, the cosmic computer, the tapestry of life. The feeling of the single origin, a oneness, the great singularity. Let's go explore this feeling, and see where it takes us.

Who are we this time?

To be distracted is to be human. Sorry, we're all very tied up at the moment. We're all too busy being human at the moment, aren't we? It was just the other day that I was standing in my editor's Manhattan office telling her that I started this new book. Yes, this is the one. I happily announced that I was writing a new book! Her assistant immediately inquired as to what is was about. I never really know what my books are to be about. -True story.

What I do know is that I was laying in bed one morning, and my spirit guides gave me the forward to this book, or at the very least, inspiration for it. So, in my usual fashion, I ran to my studio table and promptly started typing away at this book about something of which I did not know what was to be, if that makes any sense.

So, I explained to Kat, my editor, that I had written the forward to this book first. She quickly pointed out that I had, in fact, made a grave mistake, because the forward is written last and or by someone else. My rebuttal was an explanation to how I am dyslexic, and this makes perfect sense in my unique world view. I also challenged her with the thought that maybe the entire book has already been written, and that I am simply remembering what was, in fact, already written into the tapestry of time.

Again, in my mind's eye, this makes perfect sense. In fact, the Extra Terrestrials that I speak with have told me a few times that "everything is all happening at once, and there is only the present moment." Personally, I could make many arguments against this theory of theirs but I won't. I won't, because I need their help to write this book, and because I have no idea what this book is even about. Maybe it is about everything and nothing at all… we shall have to wait and see.

What I do know is that I want to talk about a great many spiritual things, bizarre things, crazy things, upside down things and of course about "THEM." Oh, and I can't forget my spirit guides. Within all these interesting subjects, my job is to somehow untie the knot that has been twisted up inside of me for the last 26 years of my life. Twisted, yes, twisted indeed. Like every other human on the face of God's green Earth. I've felt love, pain, and loss as well. Believe it or not, that is exactly why we are all here, for the pain! There is no greater teacher than pain. There are the broken hearts, divorces, deaths, break ups, beatings, failures and longings that drive our organic human machine of emotional intellect. Emotions are how we tend to filter the world that we are experiencing. It is within each year of our lives that we add another layer of experience, until it ends up looking like a stained glass window in our church of self reflection. It's very difficult to see and feel anything emotionally native if we're buried in all our little hurts.

Each layer of emotion is like an onion. Each layer will make you cry once you start peeling it back. Eventually we all have to make our way back to our center, the core of who we really are. This can unfold over many lifetimes. The heavy karmic baggage being dragged behind us needing to be healed.

Hurt and pain are interesting emotions. They are the juxtaposition of what we want and desire most. Love is the door prize for being human. The need for it is a desire to be loved and honored by all other beings in our lives. And how do we ask for LOVE when it is hidden behind a wall? A wall of pain that we won't let go of. What purpose does this serve? How do you and I untangle this mess? After realizing that, some people will just resign themselves to loving their pets because they won't ever tell you that you are really just a ruthless asshole.

The "wall" is what we run up against each time we won't let love into our hearts. That wall is what hides us from experiencing even more pain in our lives. It is so you don't ever have to step out into the light of day and get your heart broken ever again. If you only step out half way, it's so that your heart will only get half broken. In any situation, we are resigned to play it safe from here on in, after reaching adulthood. Playing it safe keeps us from ever reaching our truest potential. Playing it safe keeps you from asking out that *pretty girl, applying for that dream job or maybe writing that book you've always wanted to write.*

It's at both the beginning and end of each day that we get to look into the mirror and see what is us. Our reflection, this observation can be one of two things. It can be a mechanical and mundane thing with no love or it can be with a passion that has driven us to push ourselves even further towards success. Part of the magic is that we get to decide what the reward of success is here on Earth. It can be as simple as spending time with someone you care about or maybe something deeply complex like creating a nonprofit that rescues animals or feeds starving children. You have to first decide what is worth your time. The life clock is ticking. Notice that I didn't say making money? No matter how much money you ever have, it doesn't determine if your soul is being fulfilled and nourished.

God and or Creator did not replicate itself across the universe to make money, of that I am sure. To that point, the E.T.s that are now visiting this planet are not worried about paying their mortgages. They have no need for gas money. Think about not having to ever worry about money. This should be one consideration in working through all your spiritual goals, not ever having to worry about money. You could manifest everything that you ever needed and or desired. You are only limited by belief, nothing else.

What if we now take this conversation off the rails and talk a little about E.T.'s (extra-terrestrials). What makes them happy? Why are they wasting their time messing around with the likes of our primitive culture? Our culture that is bent on killing each other and destroying the planet with fossil fuels. Do you think that it is for their egos sake? Does ego drive them to come here? Maybe it was on a double-dog-dare to see who can pick up the most humans at night while being drunk.

My personal experience with THEM has been as crazy as a bag of cats. Sometimes I think I understand the phenomenon perfectly. But, no sooner do I feel this way... then my complete and total understanding gets destroyed by some new idea or experience. All on account of THEM.

END OF NOTES...

Tara sat there for a while reading what was to be the start of Carl's book. Carl noted how serious her face was while reading it too. He could tell that it was making her think, maybe challenging what she believed about THEM. She finally looked up at him and said,

"You always gotta be the big headed brotha, just like my dad says, huh, Carl?"

"But does it at least make sense, what I wrote?"

"Well, yes, it raises some valid points, of course. But I think it's missing something."

"What's that?"

"It's missing the love, romance, and half-naked men." And she looked at him with a mischievous smile and blew him a kiss.

"You're such a jerk. Ya' know that?" Then Tara had tears coming to her eyes from laughing so hard. She loved to get one over on him, especially when he was being way to serious. Then after she finished laughing she became a little more serious all of a sudden.

"Carl, I sort of, kind of... I want to get regressed."

"You mean hypnotized?"

"Yeah, just like you did. I want answers, Carl. Especially after that dream I had where they took my baby. I need to know if this shit is really real."

"You know it's real, Tara. You've seen THEM!" Carl's fists were now clenched, and Tara took note of it. She had triggered his anxiety.

"We all want answers, and that especially includes me."

PART IV

Try not to look...

A few years back, Carl had done some regression work with Dr. Shannon to find out what had happened to him on the boat. It was the day where he and Smitty had missing time. It had always bothered him too. He knew something wasn't right, but his young mind couldn't put the pieces together. Dr. Shannon had recorded their sessions for him to refer back to. He later let Tara listen to them. It was as if he were saying, "Are you sure you really want to be with me?" She still did, as true love accepts many faults.

"Are you really sure you want to do this, Tara? You realize that once you know, you can't not know. There are many ugly truths that I have to live with now because of my involvement with "THEM." This phenomenon sometimes doesn't make sense no matter what angle you look at it. If I had the choice of a normal life or this one, I'd choose a normal boring life. However, my soul chose this path. Now I gotta walk it; for better or worse. There is no putting the genie back it the bottle." Tara locked eyes with Carl.

"I've made up my mind, and I'm sure about this, Carl. Call Dr. Shannon and set up an appointment for me. These dreams I'm having are haunting me, night after night. I gotta know what's what."

"Okay, fine. Make sure you do a few sessions though. It takes some time to really get in deep enough, so you get all the answers." Then he asked, "Have you been hypnotized before?"

"Yes, in school by one of the performance hypnotists. I went under so easy too.

"Well, this will be different. She'll spend a good hour talking to you first and try to build a history before putting you under. It will build a direct pathway, hopefully for the answers you are seeking."

"Yes, I know. It's what I really want." Her faced appeared desperate then.

"Okay, I'll make the call."

Carl wasn't sure that this was the best idea for Tara, but he tried to be supportive nonetheless. He knew, from his experiences, that you had to relive the traumas to process what had happened. He didn't exactly find what he had hoped to find either. The answers were somewhat vague and indirect at times. The shift from Extra Terrestrial logic to Human logic was a big step.

2

On Wednesday morning both Carl and Tara drove down to Milford, where Dr. Shannon's office was. They crossed the Q Bridge again, passing where they had been rear-ended. They fought the 95 traffic all the way there.

Carl jokingly mentioned that route 95 was Connecticut's longest parking lot. After crossing the bridge, it was stop and go all the way to Milford, nothing but red lights.

Dr. Shannon's office was on the third floor of her house. It was a skinny three floor house on a postage stamp sized lot. All the houses on the street were lined up and looked exactly the same. The trade off was being so close to the beach. It was within easy walking distance.

Entering the house, Tara had the sense that this was a safe space and felt a little less tense about what was to come. But even still, the missing baby incident was at the forefront of her mind. She wanted answers, no matter what.

After a brief introduction, Carl left the office and went over to Dunkin Donuts to get some coffee and do a little drawing work. Sitting there by himself, he started to remember his own experiences again. Having seen Dr. Shannon brought up all his old memories. And so he sat there, drank coffee and drew pictures of "THEM" for the next two hours.

Back at the office, both Tara and Dr. Shannon sat down and had a long discussion about her interaction with "THEM." She wanted to know all the little details, even if they didn't seem to make any sense. Dr. Shannon had asked for dates, times and frequency. She was looking for the patterns that often emerged with abduction experiences. Most importantly, she wanted to know if there were any suspect events before the baby one. She knew that most experiencers often had lifelong contact. There was a good deal of people who had no clue this was happening to them. Abductees' minds were often clouded by screen memories, and lots of people reported seeing owls instead of the actual E.T.s. It was an endless rabbit hole of missing time and visual trickery.

Tara was finally ready. She laid back on the single-sized bed in the office. There was some ambient music playing in the background. Tara laid there with the eye covers on to block out any light. Dr. Shannon spent the next fifteen minutes talking her back to get her into a deep trance state. Tara was a good subject and went under quickly.

S: I will count to five, and at five we will be at the beginning of the night where the abduction event happened. You will just be an observer watching what is happening. There will be no pain. 1, 2, 3, even deeper, 4, and 5, we are at the beginning of the night.

T: I'm in bed reading, and then I go and see Carl. He asks me to marry him. I'm so happy! I've never been so happy. We make passionate love and eventually fall asleep together. It's very late, and we quickly fall asleep. The mood is good but my neck still hurts from the car accident.

S: Okay, you're doing very good, Tara. Now fast forward to later on in the night. What time is it that something happens? Your asleep but you can still see this. Tell me what you can see?

T: I'm asleep. It's around 2:00 or 3:00, and the room lights up. Normally this should have woken me up. I can hear a strange humming noise. Maybe it's outside. I can't move to go see it. I feel stuck, like someone is controlling me. Then, I feel like I'm laying perfectly flat, but I'm floating out through the wall somehow. This doesn't make any sense. I feel so scared! No control! Oh, God!

S: It's okay, Tara. We are only watching this. You won't get hurt. Remember, you are there as an observer. I'm counting back from five again. You are feeling more relaxed now, and more safe and more relaxed. -Now tell me what you see.

T: I'm looking around, I'm on a cold steel table. My feet are in stirrups like my OBGYN has in her office. The feeling is that I'm here for a surgery.

S: Tara, please look around. Is there anyone in the room with you?

T: Get away from me! Oh, God! What do they want? No! No! I said "No!"

S: Tara, take a deep breath and stand back so you can watch. You are only there to watch. You are safe. You are safe here in my office. No one is hurting you.

T: There are three little brown aliens with me, and their eyes are so huge. They feel so cold and unemotional. They put a needle in the back of my neck. My lower half feels numb all of a sudden. Now a big bug looking being is there. He's wearing a purple cape? I can hear him in my mind. Get out of my mind!

S: What is he telling you?

T: He says I'm done carrying their baby now. It will be okay, the child will be safe with Them. You were just a volunteer who helps us make hybrids. Life makes life.

S: Ask him if you've helped them before, Tara?

T: He says "yes," when I was a young child they harvested some of my eggs. -Tears were now rolling down her face. Dr. Shannon told her to take some more deep breaths and that she was still safe and okay. "Count back from five once more."

S: Tell me what he says next about you volunteering?

T: I'm telling him I didn't agree to this, and I want to go home. He says I volunteered for this before I was even born. Now he's saying that I was one of them in another life and so was Carl. They helped bring us together. It was meant to be. "You're both Star-Seeds."

S: Tara, what is the purpose of them making hybrids?

T: He is showing me in my mind, a picture of a rock being skipped across the water of a pond. He says "Life is like this across the known universe. It is replicating itself. It is being God, and all things are One. This is "the great singularity" he says."

S: Will they come back for you again?

T: He says not for a while, that I need time to heal. And I will get to meet my child, but he won't really look like me. We will be able to speak mind-to-mind.

S: Tell him "thanks" for all of his insight and that you are thankful that this was an informative visit to see what really happened.

T: He is touching his finger to my forehead now. All I see is rainbow light. It feels like home. So much peace. I want to be back home there.

Tara's hypnosis session lasted quite some time. She told Dr. Shannon afterwords that she felt relieved to find out about what was going on. The loss of the child was part of the agreement and was going to take some time to process and heal. A few more sessions would be needed over time so Tara could fully process what had happened.

Carl showed up after Tara messaged him. The three of them had a chance to sit down and go over some of the findings from the regression. Carl could see that

Tara looked relaxed after the session and was in a better headspace now. He wasn't sure if this therapy was going to be helpful, but now felt at the very least optimistic. Together they would now be able to move forward with their lives, no matter how unusual that might be. The truth was on the table, so to speak. And the truth, was stranger than strange is strange.

The abduction phenomenon has many facets that go well beyond our human perception. This isn't just about seeing a physical UFO in the sky. It isn't about the nuts and bolts either. These interactions can be very unsettling for many people if they are unable to embrace what they are interacting with. Many of these experiences take place in both the physical and astral bodies simultaneously. This can often make a person feel as if the interaction is only a dream. These visits from "THEM" are, in fact, very real. It's time for humanity to wake up. This new reality is coming for us all.

Part V

Situation normal, all fucked up.

"Your human mind was born unto its own constellation, Carl." Just as Carl got this message he saw an angelic figure made up of white light quickly appear and move across the room, then disappearing back into the Void. Looking up from his notes, the many objects in the room took on their own aura. The picture frame on the wall glowed at its edges. The old mirror in the fancy wooden frame glazed over like ice. The air became filled with a static noise. The room temperature suddenly felt cool. It was then that he knew for sure that he wasn't alone. The spirit world was in transit again.

The Smith family library held his fondest memories. It all at once faded into nothing. From where he sat, he could clearly see the desert sands. The wind swept across the room, making the air feel suddenly parched. Off in the distance, a lone figure stood on the furthest dune, like a spot on the sun. Here, time and space came to an end. Feature without form. Only consciousness existed. Thought with no physical distinction. Carlos suddenly spoke, "You're being watched, Carl. Watch, listen, and wait to see." The one guide who never leaves his side, always true to his cause.

The light in this space became all consuming, until nothing else existed. Carl's ears were ringing, blocking out any other noise. He couldn't think. The ringing became even more intense, then consuming his sense of sight, smell and touch. All things in view had disappeared into one singular point. Everything had been taken away. The self had ended. No ego. Carl finally had to blink trying to break the spell he was under.

Carl then opened his eyes, and quickly realized that everything was now black and yet somehow illuminated at the same time. Looking up he saw that which could not be seen. That which was never meant to be seen by a human soul. Within his mind he could see the entirety of all, the One. And it was in that space that he observed the unthinkable. This is what the old lady in the New Age store had told him about. It was she that told him that all the universes were held in perfect circles. This was God. Stepping back from himself, he could see even further. Then it transitioned until there were seven of these rings. They were laid out into a grid, like there was conscious intent to their arrangment.

The element of light shifted. His mind moved throughout space and time, moving faster and faster, and faster. The light turned into sound again and the ringing became so intense that he became dizzy. His spirit moved through the circle, through the universe, back into the Milky Way galaxy. Like a magnifying glass being held in front of his two eyes. Here he was shown the human DNA. It turned in the same spiral as the Milky Way. And in this he could see the movement of everything all at once. It was as if it was moving with conscious design and it was neatly balanced on the head of a pin. There was nothing within this that didn't begin or end without conscious intent. He saw himself there, trapped in thought. Then his mind turned within its own thoughts.

"Life. Raw, vague, and yet undiscovered. Lust. I lust to know what is even real. Lust. Do I even know what that even is?" Then the light of the room came back into focus. His silent awareness came back into his physical being with a sudden jerk. From the corner of his eye, he once again saw the spirit form that had taken him. And it began to speak softly to him.

"Reality, has been struck by the bell of time. The word reality is held in God's two hands. And do you even know what is real? A burst of energy is something that is crafted from nothing. How is something created from nothing, Carl? That emptiness that exists outside of this space and time. It is living and breathing, just as you and I are. A void that has presence of mind unto its own self." There was a long pause before it went onto say,

"The human mind, a wasteland of consumption. There, then, and in the now moment. How is any of it real? Is it "THEM" that created this reality for all of us? Ask yourself Carl. Are we living in their garden? Is the human species the tree of fertility that needs to be milked in order for all other things to exist? The only reason that you think any of this is real, is because you agree to think it is. The human machine. In perpetual motion. Even if you think that you failed Carl, you will still have succeeded. For nothing is ever lost. All lives are woven into the tapestry, never to be forgotten."

The voice slowly faded away, and Carl began to rub his eyes. The world as he knew it had come back into focus. His human machine drew in a deep breath like it had taken its very first breath. The sound of a muffled far off voice came from the doorway. "Carl, hey Carl, Earth to Carl! He finally looked up towards the intonation.

"Yes, what is it?" he looked to Tara with his lost and dazed eyes. The look on her face was that of annoyance. This situation had come to be too familiar. "I've been standing here for two minutes calling your name and you were just sitting there, staring off into nowhere. Like a zombie or something. You okay?" He took in another deep breath, feeling annoyed by her intrusion and finally said,

"Yeah, sure, I'm fine. Was just thinking. That's all."

"No, this wasn't thinking. Looked like you checked out and weren't even in your body. I was calling your name and waving my hands at you. Where did you go this time? Was it 'THEM'?"

"No, it wasn't 'THEM,' at least I don't think it was. He showed me, the desert man. You know, from the Thinking Stones story. He showed me the entirety of all the universes combined. There were seven of them, like these giant glowing rings. There was darkness, and these giant bright rings, nothing else. There's no other way to describe it. From start to finish, down to our human DNA; it was all connected. Everything came through them into being. Everything was made up of consciousness. It's all alive I tell you." Tara's face became even more serious then.

"What do you mean, it's all alive?' Did you talk to God? And who is the desert man, again? You never told me about him, did you?"

"Sure I did, and you read the book, remember." Tare then moved into the room and sat in the leather chair facing the old man's desk. "No, this is another one of your internal conversations Carl, you know, where you think you tell me things but you're only talking to yourself." He felt embarrassed, she had avoided what she knew to be true. There was no hiding it.

"Guess you're right, it was all in my head." Tara got up and walked away from the conversation abruptly. "Come to bed Carl, I need some sexy time. Put God back in his box for another day. Time to be a man again."

Feeling lost and distracted, Carl then reached for his yellow weather radio. Carl liked the prerecorded monotone female voice, "Tonight, the shoreline will experience wind gusts of forty knots. The temperature will be fourteen degrees with freezing spray. A small craft advisory has been issued." The national weather forecast covered each area of Connecticut and the Long Island Sound, too.

Still feeling lost, he opened his notebook to jot down some ideas that had suddenly taken over his thoughts. It was becoming more and more frequent to have these moments of inspiration take over his presence of mind. It was like a drug, one that had hooked into his spirit and wouldn't let go until it got its fix. Tara's request had quickly been forgotten. The beast needed to be feed.

Notes: Is any of this even real? Is the universe just one big machine, much like a computer is? Are humans just emulating God by creating and using such thinking machines? I look and I see all that is around me. Both the light and the dark. How do I know what any of it is? The only reason any of this is real, is because I think it is, if these thoughts are even my own. The human machine. I can't get this thought out of my head. An organic programmed machine where the DNA is the coding for it to run on. Just a machine. An organic container for the spirit to live through. My failure is still a success, but how? Looking back on my life, I see several versions of me that are all dead and forgotten. With each new concept, I am being reborn into someone else. So, who am I now?

Suddenly Carl was interrupted again. He felt eyes on him without even looking up to see who it even was. Tara stood in the doorway, not saying a word. She pulled the strings on her white bathrobe. Carl finally looked up. Silently she opened the robe exposing her beautiful ebony colored skin. It smelled of coco-butter. She was always telling Carl, "You better not have no ashy skin." She was beautiful and well kept. Tara exposed herself to Carl, showing her tender and very full breasts. And she had a very goddess like form, with a thin waist and large accentuated hips. Beautiful curves, that could capture any man's eye, even when clothed. Carl, forgot what he was doing just then and stared at Tara, longingly. Finally he gave in and said, "Yes, please!" and he walked away from all the business of God, DNA, the spirit world and its human machines.

Tara held her hand out to Carl, and their fingers interlocked. Flesh against flesh, man and woman defined by love. He said she "smelled beautiful" and began kissing her neck. Her long dark hair was cornrowed and easily fell back over her shoulders. He whispered into her ear, "Let's go to the bedroom baby, I need you to heal me."

Hours later, the couple were both lost in a deep sleep. During the early hours Tara became restless, and dreamed of chasing a small child down a dark hallway, trying to save it from something unseen. Carl's spirit had left his body moving into another dimension entirely. He was walking through a dark forest with huge deciduous trees that blocked out the night sky. There was a native man walking in front of him with a red tipped feather in his neatly braided hair. Moving closer, he could hear people further on down the path, talking. There was an anticipation for something good here.

The native man suddenly faded away and so he kept walking towards the voices until another man appeared in front of him. The stranger extended a hand to great him and said, "Come on, come on; they've been waiting for you." As he rounded the corner, he found himself standing at the edge of a pristine lake. The night sky was illuminating its waters. A reverse image of the sky overhead was mirrored in its reflection. People across the lake were trying to talk to him, but he instead turned his attention to the people standing directly behind him. Approaching the small group of anxious people, he made a silent greeting by opening up his two hands. Palms facing the night sky. A gesture of gratitude and humility.

Looking down, Carl's only sight was of his hands now. They appeared thinner and more brown than his normally do. His hands were held out for the others as if he were holding an invisible ball. Using his mind he then projected a hologram of the Earth. He then went onto explain through the image, how the planets axis was now at an extreme angle. This was an after effect of the "Event." The thing that ends all things. Here, the people were now living underground and letting the planet grow back into its natural state. Humanity had now finally given space back for the plants, animals and trees to exist in peace. The year was 4020 A.E. (After the Event).

From a distance, a hard buzzing noise swept through the forest. All of it melted away into a darkness. Carl, then slowly reached over stopping his alarm clock. A new day was here. It granted more opportunities of things to write about, and more information to process.

Carl, the artist and writer set about on his day. Like everyone else, he put his left foot in his left pants leg first. This particular day would be busy as he had to meet with his editor and printer in Manhattan. Like a zombie Carl appeared in the kitchen looking for toast and coffee. Tara was already dressed in her scrubs ready to go to work. Even while half asleep, Carl made note that she looked hot in her uniform. A few months ago, Tara picked up a nursing job at the hospice in Branford. This was in effort to take her mind off of what had happened with "THEM" and the missing baby. She chose instead to focus on and support others in their grief, ignoring her own. Looking to Carl, she handed him his favorite brown mug, the one that always looked dirty, even after being washed. Smiling, he reached out for the hot cup of coffee. The warmth brought him a sense of peace as the winter world raged outside. This was life, like any other January in New England. People were hiding away in their houses, waiting for Spring.

"You were very restless last night," Tara stated plainly, as if it were a common thing.

"Yeah, I imagine I was. Had a dream I was in the year 4020, after the Event."

"You mean like the Apocalypse or maybe the Rapture, just like in the Bible? You were supposed to be using that in one of your stories, right?"

"I'm not really sure how it unfolds. I was there to teach them how the planet had shifted on its axis causing this whole world to change. It was in retrospect. I couldn't see the disaster that had changed everything. It was after the fact."

"Jesus, that's some intense shit to think about first thing in the morning, Carl." She then reached over the table grabbing her hospital ID tag and put it in her pocket. Carl made note of the bar-code on it and thought about us being human machines again, or maybe walking talking computers. This idea wouldn't leave his head.

"I gotta run babe" Tara got up grabbing her lunch bag and then kissed Carl goodbye.

"Love ya," he said as she walked out the door into the sharp teeth of January's winter morning.

2

Carl set about his day with good intention. The shoreline was getting the cold winter rain, while inland got snow squalls. Dressing warm for the city he put on his black leather jump boots, cuffed blue jeans and a gray pillow down coat. He wore his old winter hat that was ripped at the seam. Like the coffee mug, he refused to let it go. These were the relics from his grandfather Smitty's life. There was comfort in their nature.

Catching the metro in New Haven, his commuter-train departed at 7:40a.m. headed for the Big Apple. For the first hour of the ride he slept with his head up against the window. The slow swaying motion always put him to sleep. Business people quietly got on and off the train until he heard the message on the loud speaker say, "Next stop 125th street, then our last stop is Grand Central station, everyone must get off the train." And as the train made it's way through the dark tunnel hidden beneath the city streets, another announcement came over the speaker. "We'll be coming in on the lower level, track 109. Please take all your trash and news papers with you." Carl thought to himself how annoyed the conductor sounded while making this announcement. One time someone had left a full coffee cup on the floor and of course it got spilled, making the bottom of his bag all wet.

Stepping off the train shadowed by the regular business people, Carl made his way out onto 42nd street. Like a herd of cows they were all shoulder to shoulder moving through the doors. The city noise came into full view. With coffee in hand, he headed east towards Lexington avenue and then took another left heading north to his publishers office.

Quietly Carl sat alone on the leather couch in the waiting room of his publishers office. Looking out the window he noted how the world outside was gray and dreary, and the world inside of his head was also stormy, confused and begotten. It was the dream, the

God experience. The one thing that had managed to break Carl's mind. To this, all of his life, there were twists and turns, which were chased by the unexplained phenomenon of "THEM." It was one concept built upon the next, as if it were on purpose somehow. Most definitely by their design.

A sharp ringing started again in his ears. Then a hot flash swept over his entire body causing him to remove the pillow coat. Consumed by the ringing noise, he found himself feeling lost. Lost in and around that one question which drives every spiritual person insane. "What is God?" Even before the ET's had made themselves known, he had started asking himself, "What is God?"

The old man had once given him really great advise, when it came to life's big questions. He said, "Keep asking yourself the same question until you get the answer, and once you have the answer, ask the question just one more time. There you will find the truth. Most people are afraid to really question life," he said. "You gotta grab it by the fucking balls and demand answers, Carl." The old man often lost site of the fact that he was speaking to a little boy.

He went onto also say, "You've always gotta fight to find the true answers to life's greater questions. People, he said, they will throw you quotes, facts, statistics and books at you. They'll shove them right into your face if you let them. A man's gotta be free to think, and all their stuff is just rubbish anyways. Only you can decide what your truth is. But if you ignore your truth, it will eventually become so loud that you can no longer ignore it. And the people who ignore their truth become sick. Sick in their spirit. I've seen many men try and ignore it. They'll try anything, sex, cars, booze, gambling; you name it. It's gonna be, what its gonna be. The truth."

Carl felt very nostalgic, missing the old man. A feeling that was a little dark and depressed, too. Unresolved emotions. The world that he was now living in felt very clouded. His mentor was no longer in it. It felt as if he were a character in someone else's play. A character that was constantly being deconstructed and then put back together again.

He then imagined himself sitting at the dinner table talking to him saying, "Sometimes, the truth is very obvious, but we somehow aren't able to reach it. Each of us is blinded with ego. This keeps people away from the opportunity of doing what is right for themselves. It's ego, Smitty. On our way to realizing this, there are three fazes of self discovery: A man is first young, then he matures finding himself becoming old, and older. Does that make sense?" The old man shook his head no and just looked away. The conversation melted into a murky haze, but it felt so real.

The double wood doors suddenly stood open. A neatly dressed women stepped out. "Carl, he will see you now." Carl followed the receptionist into John Walters office. He turned to Carl with a smile and slapped a new contract down of the table. "Go ahead, read it over, we want to work with you for another year. Your sales have been increasing month over month and you're showing great promise." John looked at the receptionist, and then back at Carl.

"You want anything to eat or drink?"

"Sure, I'll take a Coke."

"Nancy, please get the kid a Coke." And she quickly disappeared behind the wooden doors that stood guard to one man's empire. John stood at the window, watching and waiting for Carl to read over the contract. Ten minutes later, Carl finally looked up and said,

"Yeah, I guess it all looks good. Give me a pen." Then as if by magic a Coke appeared on the table in front of him. John noticed how tired Carl looked today. Feeling concerned he probed him with a few questions.

"So, what are you working on right now? Anything really creepy or maybe some more alien stories. You know, Carl, people have said to me about how good and also how original your stories are. You could be really big one day, you never know." Carl was in a daze staring out the huge plate glass windows of the office building. "Hello, Carl?" he said after a few moments of silence.

"Um, yeah… Say, John, have you ever thought about jumping out that big window?"

"Like you mean to kill yourself… like suicide?"

"No, Nothing like that man. It would be to see if any of this is really real! Haven't you ever wondered what is on the other side of this life? Maybe this reality is just one long dream. Or what if you just take over another lifetime in a parallel dimension?" John tried his best to hide the expression on his face. As he responded to Carl, he looked away.

"No, can't say that I've ever thought about that, not even a little." Carl seemed annoyed by his answer. He thought he was being deep and insightful, but the intention was lost. The world he knew, was completely different than John's. Carl looked up.

"And that's what's wrong with the world." Quickly changing the subject, John pushed him again to talk about what stories he was working on. He could clearly see that Carl was going off the rails today.

"I'm just starting to storyboard a Native American horror tale. It's about this teenage boy who takes his girlfriend to the sacred burial ground to have sex for their first time. At first she resists the idea but then eventually he wears her down until she concedes. In doing this they unleash the dark entity that was set there to protect the space. The Native Americans used "thought forms" to oversee sacred spaces. These eventually turn into their own beings. So, at night, as they lay in bed, they can hear it. The elders know right away what it is, a Roof Walker. A shaman has to be called in to perform a purification ritual after this happens."

"Sounds really good," John said with a smile. "What else you got cooking?"

"The second story is about a man who is taken by his angel to show him the destruction of the Earth, the Apocalypse. He is taken over the United States into the Midwest first, over Los Vegas, the home of sin. -The angel speaks to him and says, "Behold, the sinners shall be taken back unto the earth." Then the earth below rips open and all you see is hot lava boiling up. The train tracks and everything else are sucked in and melted. This fissure then goes all the way out to the West Coast, like a giant zipper opening up. But you get the point. Just need to work out an ending for it. I may add in a part about the dark 'Fallen' angels too."

"Huh, that sounds really cool, Carl. You're making great progress in your work, that is for sure. But one thing. Let's stay away from stories about jumping out of windows, okay." Carl gave him a half smile. He knew then that he had taken a wrong turn in their conversation.

"Thanks, I love doing this kinda' work and I've got a whole bunch more story ideas, too." After sharing his new stories, the meeting came to an end. He was on his way to becoming a well recognized comic book artist and writer. A life long dream was now being fulfilled. And he fully recognized that the impetus of all these ideas was from "THEM."

Leaving the office tower, Carl was beaming with pride. The world had shifted in his favor. Taking out his umbrella from his messenger bag he spotted a Halal cart and decided to get some lunch. Chicken Shawarma was Carl's favorite. Tara had said many times that she hated it, so he made it a point to eat it whenever he came to the city for business meetings by himself.

"Sir, Sir... Are you all right my friend? You lost or something? Carl was standing in front of the Halal cart in a daze. Hearing the man's voice, he finally snapped out of it. With some hesitation he responded.

"Why? No… I mean yes… I'm fine." Carl was acting as if nothing was wrong. The cart worker was shaking his head thinking he was on drugs or something. Not that unusual for New York city, he thought.

"You've been standing there for three minutes now. Just staring off into space."

"No, no, no... I'm okay. Was just thinking, that's all." Again, Carl got lost in his own thoughts. He thought about the God vision and the desert man. This experience had changed everything. Nothing made sense anymore. He had fallen down the proverbial rabbit hole, and never could he have imagined that it would be this deep. There wasn't a box to put any of this into either. It defied logic and left him feeling totally ungrounded. The universe was bringing him bigger and bigger concepts now as he emerged into this new person. Like always, he thought it was all because of "THEM."

Walking back to the train-station, he was the human machine. Automatic and thoughtless in his motion. And before he even started his day, the phenomenon was after him. Carl had gotten a message as he wiped the moisture off of the bathroom mirror exposing his image. The message from "THEM" was still the same. "Promise, the promise, you promised to tell the story." He stopped and contemplated if this was even real or was he completely losing his shit?

"What if this reflection of me isn't even real? Maybe someday, I'll just wake up and see that this was all a dream. All my life, I've felt like I've been held underwater. I keep trying to push my way to the surface and come up for air, but I can't. It is the dream within the dream. An endless loop where there is no escape. Reality is the great illusion. Fuck, I gotta wake up! And my presence of mind. This reality matrix is like some giant computer program. A system built to enslave the mind. The only reason that any of this is real, is because I agree to it. A trap. A system that is another man's dream, a soul prison." Carl's spirit guide then interrupted his metal chatter.

"Even if you fail, you will still have succeeded Carl. Remember that." Carl then nodded in agreement.

3

Moving through the revolving door, a kaleidoscope of brass and glass, Carl had now made his way back to the train station. He caught a peak hour train, the 4:52 train to New Haven. While entering track 19, he noted how naked and raw the tunnels were. This was the true city, filled with steam pipes, cables, wires and numbered doors that people weren't aloud to go through. Concrete without the facade of money.

After the conductor had taken his ticket, he put his music on, laid his head against the window and quickly dozed off. After Harlem, 125th street, he was awakened by a strange face seen only in his minds eye. There was no voice or message to it, just this face. It was its appearance that had startled him. It didn't look like any of "THEM" either. It had the peach colored skin of angels. The complexion was of someone who was of Irish decent and was covered in tiny freckles. The eyes were most disconcerting though. They were yellow in black, and appeared to be almost cat like. Carl wondered if this was somehow a hybrid of a human, an ET and an angel. It seemed possible to him, just maybe? How could anyone really know how many versions of the hybrids were out in the universe, anyway.

He kept thinking about it until the train crossed the Williams bridge. Looking out the window at the sea of gray mist, he spotted something unusual. "No, it can't be!" Just over the East River was a UFO craft suspended in mid-air, just sitting there, like a parked car. Out in plain sight. Carl quickly looked around the train and then back at it. In this moment, time appeared to slow down somehow. Thinking he wasn't alone in seeing this craft he then stood up and looked around the car again at the other passengers. They stared back at him with a blank gaze. "They're all zombies," he thought. Sitting back down he kept watch until the train was to far off to see it any longer. The moment faded back into the wet cold January gray.

Carl assumed that the face must have been an occupant of the UFO. Why else would he have seen it? It had purposely woken him up, too. There had to be some sort of cause and effect at work here. Nothing that he saw was by chance. It all had purpose, an intelligent design. "Clearly I'm being watched, but who are they? Things are about to shift again. I can feel it. Something is coming for me." The hair on the back of his neck stood up then and a cold chill swept over him. Even if the mind denied it, the physical body knew what was real. And then he heard the old mans voice in his head saying, "Carl, always trust your gut."

Once the train had made it to Stamford station, Carl was woken up again. This time by a loud voice on the intercom. "We apologize for the delay... all riders will have to get off the train now... there was a suicide strike in Norwalk. Trains are be rerouted, you will have to listen for the announcement for the next available train leaving the station. This may take a few hours folks. We apologize for the delay." Carl reached into his bag for his phone.

The phone rings. Tara rushed to answer it, walking away from doing her laundry. She didn't have enough scrubs to make it through the work week. It seemed like everyday was laundry day.

"Hello."

"Hey babe, it's me."

"Carl, are you okay?" Tara's voice showed that she was very worried about him, but didn't know why. It was pure instinct. She always seemed to know if something was not quite right with her Carl. A not yet identified level of perception that she was destined to open up to. Contact with "THEM" had that effect on people, whether they wanted it or not. Tara could hear lots of people talking in the background on her end of the line. Carl took a deep breath before speaking. She could tell he was agitated.

"Babe, I'm fine. Some idiot jumped in front of the train killing themselves up in Norwalk. Now I'm stranded here in Stamford for a few hours while they investigate the crime seen. Talk about bad luck. It's never just a few hours! Remember last summer when my train got stuck in the August heat? The fucking worst! Metro-North and it's antiquated overhead power lines. Bah!" Tara felt a little relief after hearing Carl's voice. At least he was okay, she thought.

"Do you want me to drive down there and pick you up?"

"No, it will take you two hours in rush hour traffic to get here. I'll take a cab up to Bridgeport and take the train from there back to New Haven. Hopefully I'll get home by seven or eight. We'll see."

"Oh, all right, I'm gonna work on taking down the office wall paper so we can paint this weekend.

"Sounds good to me," Carl said flatly.

"Oh, and before I forget, we got the insurance check from the lawyer today. Who could forget the car accident. I know my back hasn't. And it's a lot of money Carl."

"Wow, I never thought it would come. Shit took forever! I'll deposit it at the bank tomorrow, then we can pay your car off." The conversation ended there as Carl's phone dropped the signal for some unknown reason. He quickly texted Tara back, "I love you babe."

Carl pulled into the driveway at around quarter to eight later that evening. Feeling exhausted he dropped his messenger bag by the door, threw his coat on the kitchen chair and grabbed a beer. He made himself a quick ham and cheese sandwich and headed upstairs to see how Tara was doing with the remodel work. He rounded the corner to the library.

"Hey babe, I'm back." Tara was on her knees at the edge of the wall. She had a vacant look on her face. In her hand was a group of black and white photos. In front of her was a stack of faded yellow envelopes. She didn't even look at him, and just raised her hand to give Carl the photo's. These were old photos from the fifties of an alien autopsy. "Carl, what the fuck. I can't unsee this!" He then noticed that there was a section of the wall missing. The old man had buried these in the wall and sealed it in with cardboard and then wallpapered over it. Tara put out her hand for Carl's and he helped her to her feet.

"He must have known that you would find this Carl!" But he didn't quite know what to think just then. It was all too much. This was hard, even for him to believe.

"I Guess, maybe, on some level he did. Or maybe not. Who the hell knows. Maybe someone else was supposed to get them, and then he decided against it. I'm at a loss."

For the next two hours both Carl and Tara sat on the floor looking through the photo's and notes that went with them. At one point Carl looked to Tara and said, "There must be at least twenty different species of ET's here. Where the fuck did they all come from? How did they get here? I have so many questions!" Tara then looked at him and just shook her head. She finally got up and said, "I'm gonna need something stronger to drink if we're gonna keep looking at these Carl. You want a whiskey?"

"Yeah, please. With ginger-ale, too. Thanks" Carl started making separate piles after this and tried to organize them by date and by what he thought were different species. In his mind he was smiling as none of the notes were redacted, unlike the UFO books that he had seen in the New Age store.

Hours had passed. Both Carl and Tara organized all that they could on this very strange night. After, the piles were put away into an old plastic milk crate. Carl often stole these crates from the local convenience store to hold his artwork and comics. Tara always said that he was so "ghetto" when he came home with them.

As soon as their heads hit the pillow, they both fell into a deep sleep. They had exhausted themselves with the excitement of this new find. Carl couldn't wait until tomorrow came so he could start working through the notes. His imagination wondered as he drifted off to sleep. There were many imaginings of him trying to create a new story from them.

4

In the city, the world outside was dark, gray, complex and haunted by an unseen force. The world inside of this space was torn, confused and begotten; no one knew why. People moved in and out of the shadowy spaces that no one dared to speak of. The city held a veneer that said it was "beautiful, successful and rich," turning a blind eye to its true self. It was built upon the backs of the weak. Brick by brick, and life by life.

In the borough of Queens, many lives were consumed by this violent and unseen force. There were those who called the shots, those who preyed upon the weak and those who were never spoken of, for fear of what may come there after. Here, even the monsters had monsters. Every dark soul had its' own demon, a puppet master, making it sing. If you wanted the real truth, you would have to enter this space. The good and the righteous had adapted to exploit the darkness when it served their purpose. Gods angels had also adapted to survive here among the Fallen. They too played their own game of good versus evil, waiting for just the right moment, to begin again.

Many of the industrial buildings here in Queens looked much the same. Red and tan bricks, rusted garage doors, corrugated metal, and broken bottles on the sidewalks. A secrecy among the unkempt structures. Hidden in plane sight, but no one would look up to see it.

Standing amongst the others was a vacant two story building that was girdled by barbed wire and tattooed with spray painted murals depicting city street life. No one was ever seen coming or going from it. Tonight was to be an exception.

The rusted garage door to this building had painted numbers on it, 45-454. And it was at precisely 1a.m. that the door had finally opened for what seemed to be the first time. There wasn't a single soul there to witness this. A large silver truck rolled out. On the side of the truck was the iconic logo for "Wonder Bread." It was not unusual to see these type of trucks in the early part of the morning making their rounds, picking up goods from the bread factories.

Through the darkened streets, fog hung low and spitting rain fell. The bread truck made it's way slowly to the entrance ramp of rout 687, then to I-95 North towards Connecticut. The truck slowly lumbered through up state New York, eventually making it to Fairfield county. The truck rolled through each toll station never having to stop. It was followed by an unseen force. The two occupants wore black one piece jumpers and black leather gloves. Their hats and uniforms were identical. Their facial features blank. They looked almost human with a chalky skin tone. They too were both cold and expressionless. Void of any feelings. Robotic in nature. Mechanical in their movements. Operating under the direction of those who were the puppet masters to Earths garden. Change was wanted, and they moved their pawns to make it happen. The next time cycle was in the works, both the light and dark were taking up their positions to fight the unseen war. The war of who controlled humanity.

The bread truck exited I-95 moving into the sleepy bedroom town of Branford Connecticut. Moving through its streets, all the traffic lights were turning green. Going down Main street, the truck took a sharp right turn at the town green and it then had to reroute to avoid the train underpass. Finally making its way to Branford Point, it took a right onto Linden avenue. Moving slowly parallel to the waters edge, the truck finally turned right onto Bayberry lane. As the silver bread truck crept through the beach front community, the power slowly went out, blacking out every home and street light. The beach front neighborhood had erupted into an unknown silence.

Both Carl and Tara were dead asleep. Carl dreamt of a motor running outside of their modest beach front home. The noise was a low hum, droning on and on. Two dark figures were parked out front, with the motor still running. They quietly opened the back doors of their truck and moved out Carl's old sea chest. The two occupants were being methodical, so not to bump or disturb its contents. They left it at the backdoor with a simple note attached.

"Thought you might need this back. There's still room in it for your other files, too. We will be watching with great anticipation."
-The Watchers

For more information about Craig Lefebvre visit:
www.dimensional-healings.com
e-mail: Dimensional.healingsCT@gmail.com

Other titles by Craig Lefebvre:
The Vessel of ONE
Blue Star Prophecy
The Cube Life
WHISPER HEAD Poetry
Abductee Poetry
The Alien Abduction Survival Journal
Button Factory Manifesto